D1562356

CHILD'S PLAY

Kerri walked silently over to the window and looked out on the deserted street. The rain had softened to a mist which made rainbow halos around the streetlights.

She touched the glass and warmed it, feeling the power in her fingertips.

What first, she thought.

Outside the streetlights began to flicker and she watched dispassionately as the one nearest the house went dark.

Not good enough.

In rapid succession, three of the globes exploded, showering blue-white sparks onto the wet pavement as fragments of glass whistled through the air.

She turned her gaze toward the more distant lights.

Alternating from one side of the street to the other, the streetlights disintegrated in a flurry of white flashes.

It was beautiful.

And it was only the beginning . . .

THRILLERS & CHILLERS
from Zebra Books

DADDY'S LITTLE GIRL   (1606, $3.50)
by Daniel Ransom
Sweet, innocent Deirde was missing. But no one in the small quiet town of Burton wanted to find her. They had waited a long time for the perfect sacrifice. And now they had found it . . .

THE CHILDREN'S WARD   (1585, $3.50)
by Patricia Wallace
Abigail felt a sense of terror form the moment she was admitted to the hospital. And as her eyes took on the glow of those possessed and her frail body strengthened with the powers of evil, little Abigail—so sweet, so pure, so innocent—was ready to wreak a bloody revenge in the sterile corridors of THE CHILDREN'S WARD.

SWEET DREAMS   (1553, $3.50)
by William W. Johnstone
Innocent ten-year-old Heather sensed the chill of darkness in her schoolmates' vacant stares, the evil festering in their hearts. But no one listened to Heather's terrified screams as it was her turn to feed the hungry spirit—with her very soul!

THE NURSERY   (1566, $3.50)
by William W. Johnstone
Their fate had been planned, their master chosen. Sixty-six infants awaited birth to live forever under the rule of darkness—if all went according to plan in THE NURSERY.

SOUL-EATER   (1656, $3.50)
by Dana Brookins
The great old house stood empty, the rafter beams seemed to sigh, and the moon beamed eerily off the white paint. It seemed to reach out to Bobbie, wanting to get inside his mind as if to tell him something he didn't want to hear.

Available wherever paperbacks are sold, or order direct from the Publisher. Send cover price plus 50¢ per copy for mailing and handling to Zebra Books, Dept. 1766, 475 Park Avenue South, New York, N.Y. 10016. DO NOT SEND CASH.

TWICE BLESSED

BY PATRICIA WALLACE

ZEBRA BOOKS
KENSINGTON PUBLISHING CORP.

ZEBRA BOOKS

are published by

Kensington Publishing Corp.
475 Park Avenue South
New York, NY 10016

Copyright 1986 by Patricia Wallace

All rights reserved. No part of this book may be repro-
duced in any form or by any means without the prior
written consent of the Publisher, excepting brief quotes
used in reviews.

First printing: February 1986

Printed in the United States of America

For Helen
and
For Andy

"The life of children, as much as that of intemperate men, is wholly governed by their desires."

Aristotle

"Children are completely egoistic; they feel their needs intensely and strive ruthlessly to satisfy them."

Sigmund Freud

Prologue

It was raining . . .

Eyes closed, Edana Morgan felt the rain as it splashed on her eyelids, forming cold tears which mixed with her own and ran down her face. She licked her lips, tasting not the salt of tears, but the metallic flavor of blood.

Her blood? Or her husband's?

"Peter," she whispered, and remembered. The headlights cutting through the dark, wet night, the car sliding on the rain-slick road, turning until it was sideways and then—almost in slow motion—slamming into the trees.

Peter's face, bloodied and pale in the dim light.

A sudden pain, hot and piercing, spread through the fullness of her abdomen, and she gasped, arching her back. Searing waves of rock-hard pain . . . a wrenching pull in her belly . . . a gush of warm liquid from between her legs.

"Help me," she pleaded, trying to bring her knees up, but her legs were trapped under the seat, and she

9

whimpered as something twisted loose inside her.

The last thing she heard as she slipped from consciousness was the wail of a siren as it split the night air.

"Jesus," someone exclaimed as the woman was brought into the trauma room.

Willow Thompson looked up from the I.V. tray and frowned. After five years as a nurse in the emergency department, she had come to believe that the worst thing that could happen to a patient was to know how badly they were hurt. She also believed that, conscious or not, the patient was somehow able to hear, and if what they heard was bad enough, sometimes they just gave up.

In this emergency department, on her shift, careless talk was not tolerated.

But as she got her first clear view of the patient, she silently echoed the thought: *Jesus!*

Thick, dark blood was matted in the woman's hair and her face was streaked with it. Tiny splinters of glass adhered to the sticky surfaces, while other larger fragments seemed to be embedded in flesh. A gash along the jaw line gaped open, showing the white of bone and oozing blood. Frothy pink bubbles of blood and saliva collected at the corners of her mouth.

But it was not the face which held her attention.

Beneath the gray blanket, the woman's abdomen was swollen in pregnancy, its fullness unmistakable and somehow frightening.

Willie pushed the thought from her mind; there

was no time for such foolishness.

She moved to the bedside and began to work quickly, her slim brown fingers locating a vein in the patient's arm and positioning the needle. Puncturing the skin, she maneuvered the needle until she felt a slight *pop* as it entered the vein. Blood welled from the base of the intracath, and she attached the intravenous line, checking to make sure there were no crimps in the tubing, and then taped the needle in place.

"Peter," the woman moaned.

Willie paused, looking at her patient, but there was no awareness in that ashen, ruined face.

Just as well, Willie thought.

Shadows played across the woman's battered features as they pushed the gurney down the dimly lit hallway toward the operating room. The orderly whistled softly through his teeth.

"Can it," Willie ordered.

"Yes'm." He began to hum.

She gave him an annoyed look, then turned her attention back to the patient. They had a name now—Edana Morgan. Age twenty-two and newly widowed, according to the police officer who had arrived with what he called "the effects"; a blood-stained leather purse complete with identification and other remnants of the young woman's life.

They neared the entrance to the surgical holding area and Willie smacked the metal pressure plate which activated the double doors.

A sharp antiseptic odor assailed her nostrils and

11

she breathed through her mouth, envying the surgery nurses the cloth masks they wore.

"Whew," the orderly muttered, "they must be killing germs by asphyxiation . . ."

Under the bright lights, Edana Morgan's face was the color of death and only the high-pitched tones of the heart monitor gave proof of her survival. Willie reached out and tucked a strand of dark hair—still stiff with blood—under the surgical cap.

"Is this our c-section?" One of the surgery nurses had come up beside them, her manner, like all operating room nurses Willie had ever met, like that of an army sergeant; disinterested but somehow challenging.

"Among other things," Willie answered. She took a step back from the gurney and handed over the thin packet of paperwork which comprised the patient's chart. "I went over the pre-op checklist with the nursing supervisor in E.R.; everything's in order."

"That would be a nice change."

Willie recognized condescension when she heard it, and she heard it now. She looked at the surgical nurse, who she felt sure wouldn't last ten minutes in the frantic disorder of the emergency room, and smiled.

"We try," she said mildly.

At twenty past two in the morning, the emergency department finally emptied and quiet, Willie stopped the anesthesiologist who was on his way home.

"How's Mrs. Morgan?"

"Who?" He looked at her tiredly and then glanced

12

at his watch. "Which . . . ?"

"The c-section."

"Ah." He nodded, pursing his lips. "Very lucky to get that one through the surgery. She went into tachycardia about half-way through."

"And the baby?"

"Babies." He drew a graying handkerchief out of his pocket and wiped it across his forehead. "Fraternal twins . . . a boy and a girl."

"Oh!" Willie had listened to the fetal heartbeat; she would have sworn that she'd only heard one . . .

"It'll be a miracle if either of them makes it, though." He started toward the exit. "Too damned small."

When she got off duty at eight a.m., Willie went up to the fifth floor neonatal intensive care unit. The NICU had only been in service for two months and its very newness was like a badge of optimism.

Admittance to the unit was restricted—personnel and visitors were screened via a closed circuit television system before gaining entrance through a magnetically-locked door—so she walked along the glass-enclosed nursery until she came to the critical care area where the most seriously ill newborns were cared for.

There were five babies inside, each in an Isolette surrounded by monitors and life support equipment. Two of them were much smaller than the others, and she felt a sudden ache as she looked at them.

So tiny.

They lay naked, thin limbs splayed, wired and

harnessed to the machinery. Umbilical catheters dripped precious fluid into their veins and oxygen was gently forced into underdeveloped lungs. The array of technology included peripheral intravenous lines for the administration of antibiotics; a transcutaneous peripheral oxygen monitor; blood pressure monitor; and electrodes for heart and respiration rate. Each baby's eyes were patched as protection against ultraviolet lamps which bathed them in light.

The unit was soundproofed, but Willie could hear in her mind the hiss of the respirators, the high-pitched tones of all those monitors, the piercing undulation of electronic alarms.

An alien environment.

She pressed closer to the glass and realized that she was holding her own breath even as she counted each of theirs. How long would their immature lungs be able to oxygenate their blood, even with the help of the respirators?

Looking at them, Willie was forced to agree with the anesthesiologist; it would take something very near a miracle for them to survive.

When she returned to work after two days off, she asked after the Morgan twins.

"Oh yes," the nursing supervisor said, nodding. "They're holding their own so far."

Willie closed her eyes, overwhelmed by a feeling of relief and something else. Something not as easily defined.

The nursing supervisor continued to talk, but Willie heard none of it.

Instead she looked inward, trying to determine the source of her apprehension. Was it the uncertainty as to whether the twins would somehow manage to elude the maladies common to premature babies—cerebral hemorrhage, respiratory collapse, immune system failure—and beat the odds against their survival?

". . . the best medical care," the nursing supervisor was saying.

Willie hesitated only slightly. "Yes," she agreed, "and by the grace of God."

In the mornings, after work, Willie would go up to the fifth floor and stand at the window, watching them.

She had her own reasons . . . deep, personal reasons . . . for wanting them to live.

Their mother named them. The girl was called Kerri and the boy, Galen.

Edana Morgan, looking fragile and very young, took her children home on a clear morning in May.

They were sixteen weeks old.

Chapter One

Edana stood at the sink, watching water fill the cast iron pot she always used for spaghetti, only half-listening to the children's voices from upstairs.

Sounds carried in the old wood frame house, traveling along the narrow hallways and echoing in darkened corners like distant thunder. It was difficult to distinguish words—in fact she seldom tried—but usually she could detect an impending crisis by tone and volume.

They had had more than their share of crises lately, a fact she attributed to the long hours she was putting in studying for the upcoming nursing exams. The children acted as mirrors, reflecting her stress, but for now, at least, all seemed calm.

She turned off the water and carried the pot to the stove, placing it on a back burner. Hamburger was browning in a skillet to one side.

The clock above the stove showed just past five o'clock.

"No!"

Startled, Edana looked up at the ceiling. Galen? He was the more even-tempered of the two, the peacemaker. It was unlike him to raise his voice, even when provoked.

A door slammed upstairs and footsteps sounded on the stairs.

Edana reached the front hall in time to see her son throw open the front door and run out of the house, the screen door clattering shut behind him.

"Galen."

He did not turn at the sound of her voice, but hurried toward the sidewalk, hands thrust deep in his pockets in a gesture so much like his father that for a moment she was seeing Peter . . .

A rustling noise distracted her and she turned to see Kerri standing in the shadows at the top of the stairway.

For a heartbeat, Edana had an impression of something cold passing by her, a frigid rush of air extending out of the house toward where Galen stood in the fading sunlight.

"Kerri, what is it?"

Her daughter's blue eyes flickered, a hint of a smile playing across her delicate face.

Edana looked back outside where Galen stood at the curb as if waiting. Taking a step toward the door, Edana was struck still as her son suddenly whirled and faced the house.

"No!" he screamed and then—

This can't be happening!

—took a step off the curb into the street.

Edana heard the car before she saw it, and she was

18

moving, her palms smacking into the screen door, flinging it open, but as she ran onto the porch she knew it was too late, heard the screech as the brakes locked, heard the dull thump of metal as it struck that sturdy little body, watched her child thrown into the air by the force of impact, watched as he came to earth in a boneless heap, watched as he lay motionless in the absolute silence which followed.

This isn't real, her mind protested, and she looked back to where Kerri had been standing, expecting to see both of her children . . . her golden-haired son, her darkly pretty daughter.

But Kerri was gone and Galen lay crumpled in the street.

Edana knelt beside her son, her reluctant eyes taking in the dark wet blood in his hair and the raw surface of his skin where it had scraped against the pavement. She saw, too, the swelling along the side of his head and the thin trickle of blood from his left ear.

Around her she heard the excited murmur of voices and her fingers shook as she pressed them into the soft warmth of his throat, searching for a pulse.

He was still alive.

Without taking her eyes from his face, she reached over and grabbed the arm of one of the bystanders.

"An ambulance," she ordered.

"On the way," a man's voice answered.

There was nothing she could do but wait, listening for the sound of her nightmares . . . the siren as it neared.

Again, she thought.

Chapter Two

The pager went off just as Dr. Megan Turner pulled onto the freeway on-ramp. At five-thirty on a Friday afternoon, the traffic was barely moving, tied up, she suspected, not by an accident, but by last-minute lane changers.

With a glance in the rear-view mirror, she maneuvered the car to the right, driving along the shoulder toward the next exit. Luck was with her; the lane, reserved for breakdowns, was clear all the way to the off-ramp.

In less than five minutes she was pulling into the parking lot of Valley Memorial Hospital. An ambulance, its doors gaping open, was backed up to the emergency entrance. A fire rescue truck was parked to one side, bracketed by police cars. An accident, then.

By the time she made her way through the cluster of paramedics, firemen and cops, she knew that the victim was a child, and that it was bad.

"Megan." Dave Levine's voice boomed from behind her, and she turned just as the chief of emergency services, all five foot four, two hundred pounds of him, pushed through to her side.

"What've you got?"

"Personally? Nothing contagious." Then he grimaced, the smile fading from his face. "Seven year old boy with a head injury, internal bleeding. The neurosurgeon's in with him now and the belly man is on the way." Levine rubbed his own ample midsection. "You're on call for admissions."

Megan nodded. "What happened?"

"Auto versus pedestrian, with the usual outcome."

"Is there family?"

"The mother's here somewhere . . ."

"Do we have a history yet?"

"I left that for you, darlin'." His smile reappeared. "Lord knows you won't be able to get within yards of the boy until the specialists have finished specializing."

"Right." She looked at the bedlam surrounding her, amazed as always that such seeming disorder could produce the medical miracles which were everyday occurrences here.

Megan disregarded Levine's advice and made her way into the trauma room. It was important, since she was going to go talk to the boy's mother, that she have an accurate idea of how he was doing. As admitting physician, she was ultimately responsible for his medical care, but during the acute emergency stage of treatment, with surgical and trauma specialists orchestrating the life-saving measures, her responsibilities were as much to the family as the patient.

Galen Morgan lay naked on the gurney. His clothes had been cut off and were piled in a heap in the

22

corner.

According to the chart, he had been comatose on arrival after sustaining blunt trauma to the head. He had undergone an emergency tracheotomy on arrival in E.R. and was on a respirator. Sandbags on either side of his neck held his head still. Intravenous lines were established in the right subclavian artery and via a cutdown above the left ankle. The x-rays of his skull, chest and abdomen were lined up on the light boxes which covered most of one wall. A cardiac monitor recorded his heart rate.

One of the nurses gently debrided the road burns across his face and chest while another prepared to catheterize him. A third adjusted the flow of IV fluids.

The neurosurgeon—Dr. Abrahms—stood at the head of the gurney, shining a light into the boy's eyes and frowning at what he saw there.

But what Megan saw was the child's hands, cupped and relaxed as if he were only sleeping, soon to wake. She moved to the side of the bed and reached to stroke the small fingers.

One of the nurses saw and smiled sadly.

"He's a beautiful child," the nurse said.

Megan looked at Galen's face, his features, in repose, so symmetrical as to near perfection, marred only slightly by the raw patches of abraded skin. "Yes," she said, "isn't he?"

She conferred briefly with Dr. Abrahms and then started down the hallway.

A voice called after her, "Dr. Turner."

"Yes?" One of the other nurses who had been caring for Galen caught up to her, and began walking

23

alongside.

"You're going to talk with Mrs. Morgan?"

"I am."

"I don't know if anyone's mentioned it to you, but Edana . . . Mrs. Morgan . . . is in her final semester of nursing school."

"No, I wasn't aware of that."

"I thought I'd better tell you, because, you know, she's going to have some ideas about what's been going on."

"Ideas?"

The nurse hesitated. "Knowledge can be a dangerous thing . . . most people, when something happens to someone in their family, are blessedly ignorant of what really goes on in a hospital. They half-remember what they've seen on TV, which is pretty mild compared to what actually happens."

Megan nodded; as a resident, on those rare occasions when it was quiet enough on the floors to allow a few minutes of relaxation, the medical shows were the programs of choice. Comic relief, as it were, from the realities of medicine. Those heroic, immaculate, self-possessed doctors were always good for a laugh. And the medicine practiced . . . never before had so little effort saved so many lives so quickly.

"What I'm saying," the nurse continued, "is that Edana knows how bad this is. She might not be thinking clearly right now, but eventually her nurse's training will catch up with her, and then she's going to imagine the worst, simply because she *knows* what the worst is."

They were nearing the quiet room where Edana Morgan was waiting.

"You're right, of course."

"So when she asks, tell her the truth. All of it. No matter how bad it is."

Megan hesitated only briefly, then nodded a second time. "I'll tell her . . . when she asks."

Chapter Three

Edana tried not to look at her watch, knowing that only minutes had passed since she'd checked before, both anxious for and dreading the passage of time.

They had put her in the quiet room.

Four months shy of completing her training, she knew what being made to wait in the quiet room meant; Galen was in critical condition. She had been ushered into the windowless room by a dour-faced woman who avoided meeting her eyes.

"Someone will come talk to you soon," the woman said, and closed the sliding door to deter any questions.

A policeman had been in, apologetically explaining that he had no news of her son, but reassuring her that one of the neighbors was looking after her daughter and the house had been locked up.

She'd felt a moment of guilt; Kerri. She'd forgotten about Kerri. Had she seen what happened to Galen? The two of them were so close . . . what would happen to Kerri if . . .

No.

She wouldn't even think that.

Determinedly, she tried to concentrate on what the policeman was saying, but . . . he was gone, as silently and quickly as he'd appeared, and she had a nagging feeling that she'd missed something, missed some vital piece of information, some clue as to what was going on.

So she waited. Pacing, closing her eyes against the images which flooded her mind.

Galen, his head striking the pavement.

The paramedics working feverishly over the still form of her son as she stood aside, helpless.

The crimson stain on the road, where his head had lain, after they lifted him onto the stretcher.

Curious faces watching as the ambulance pulled away.

The last glimpse, as he was wheeled into emergency and was surrounded by the nurses and doctors who would fight for his life.

She found herself looking at her watch.

It was nearly seven.

The door slid open behind her and she turned, aware all at once of the pounding of her heart. A dark-haired woman wearing a white lab coat over a pale blue dress, stethoscope tucked in one pocket, stood in the doorway.

"Mrs. Morgan?"

Edana nodded, unable to speak.

"I'm Dr. Turner. They've taken your son into surgery . . ."

She had signed the consent forms, signed them without reading, signed one after the other, the words of explanation offered by the admitting nurse somehow meaningless. "Surgery?"

The doctor looked at her intently. "Maybe you'd better sit down."

Edana allowed herself to be guided into a chair.

After a moment, the doctor continued: "Your son . . . Galen . . . has a subdural hematoma from the head injury, and his brain is swelling. The neurosurgeon, Dr. Abrahms, has drilled burr holes in his skull and he's receiving diuretics to help reduce the edema, and anticonvulsants to prevent seizures."

"Oh God."

"They're preparing to do an exploratory laparotomy to determine the cause of the abdominal bleeding, and then they'll do whatever they can to stop it."

Edana held tightly onto the arms of the chair. "Tell me," she forced the words through parched lips, "is he dying?"

"He's holding his own so far."

Hot tears blurred her vision and she struggled for control. "But he's so little . . ."

Dr. Turner reached across and gripped her hand. "Cry if you need to. You don't have to be strong all of the time."

"My bright little one," Edana whispered after a while, her throat aching from her tears. She looked up to see the doctor watching her. "Galen . . . means bright little one in Gaelic." She swallowed hard. "And he is . . ."

"Yes."

"I'm afraid," Edana said.

"I know."

"When I saw him that way, all battered, I was more frightened than I've ever been in my life." She shuddered at the memory, then sought to compose

28

herself, grateful for the doctor's supportive silence. "I wanted to be a nurse because of Galen and Kerri and their father . . . I wanted to help other people the way that we were helped. And I think I'm a good nurse. But when it was my son, when it was Galen . . . I was terrified. I didn't want to know what I know. I couldn't bring myself to look in his eyes and see . . ."

"I understand."

"Do you? Because I don't." Her anguish threatened to overwhelm her. "I've been going crazy wondering if all of this is to save a little boy who . . . who is already gone from me. Going crazy because I didn't look to see if his pupils were dilated and fixed . . . if he's brain dead . . . if there's a chance . . ."

"There *is* a chance," Dr. Turner said.

"I want to believe you."

"We're doing amazing things in medicine these days . . . there's always a chance."

Edana looked into guileless hazel eyes.

"All right," she said then, "tell me everything."

Later, when she'd listened to all there was to hear, she answered questions about Galen's medical history, detailing as well as she could the early days after his birth when, as now, he'd hovered between life and death.

And when she was alone again, she prayed.

Chapter Four

At nine fifty-five p.m., the unit secretary in intensive care hung up the phone and announced, "Ten minutes."

"Damn and double-damn," Rita Cortez cursed under her breath. It never failed; no matter how quickly she worked, no matter how much warning she had, she was never quite ready when a new admit arrived.

This one was coming directly from surgery which in itself was a bad sign; only the most critical patients bypassed the recovery room and were brought straight to the unit.

A seven year old boy with a head injury and newly minus a spleen.

Rita sighed and leaned over, wiping down the side rails of the bed with ethyl alcohol. As a nurse it wasn't her job to clean up, but having lost a few patients to hospital-acquired infections, she felt better if she did it.

Housekeeping tried, but most of them were intimidated by the machinery and maze of connecting wires and lines which surrounded each bed. Patients like

Mr. Snyder, who had occupied bed one for almost seven weeks, lay in beds encrusted with filth. Urine leaked from catheters, stomach contents spilled from nasogastric tubes, airborne particulates coughed up from diseased lungs . . . it made her sick to think about it.

No one else seemed to mind, particularly not Mr. Snyder, who stared with unseeing eyes at the ceiling, his toothless mouth open, his fetid breath fouling the air around him.

She had never been assigned to Mr. Snyder . . . yet. She was more than a little phobic about cleanliness, which she personally rated a step above godliness, but just in case she crossed herself as she turned from the bed.

Any minute now.

The boy arrived at exactly five after ten and she knew it was going to be a long night.

Barely visible among the tangle of cables and monitor lead wires connecting him to the telemetry and life support equipment, he resembled a discarded puppet. His skin looked pale and waxy under the harsh fluorescent lights.

Rita accepted the chart handed to her by one of the surgery nurses and stood back out of the way as the transport team prepared to move the child onto the bed. First they had to switch the monitoring leads from the portable machines to the ICU systems which were up and running straight lines.

The others were so engrossed in hooking the correct lines to the correct machines that they didn't see.

When the boy was plugged into the computerized life support system, the LED displays lit up like a Christmas tree.

A power surge?

Rita took a step forward just as the lights flickered overhead.

"Not again," someone groaned.

There had been a black-out two days before. The hospital was equipped with emergency generators in case of power failure, but the brief interval it took for the switch from main to back-up power was all that was needed to trigger dozens of alarms on the life support systems. It was decidedly nerve-wracking, waiting in the dark for the lights to come on while a cacophony of alarms sounded.

But this time the lights only faded and then came up again, and in a minute it was forgotten.

Rita drew the curtains just enough to isolate the boy from the patients on either side of him. ICU was not renowned for affording its patients privacy, but the thought of leaving the youngster on view disturbed her. And, perhaps, she wanted to shield him from the spectacle of others dying around him.

Not that he could see them.

She pulled the clean white sheet up to his chest and wondered if he could feel the cool fabric against his skin. It was a small comfort, but—entwined as he was with the lines and tubes which anchored him to the machines—she thought it a welcome one.

It took almost forty-five minutes for her to do her work-up, and by the time she'd finished checking for infiltrated IV lines, changed the surgical dressings, and administered his medications, Rita realized that she was not going to be very objective about this child.

Despite the tenet that emotional attachment to a patient could be counterproductive, Rita was hooked.

"Galen," she said softly, watching for any response. There was none.

Chapter Five

When she came across it on the census sheet, Willie Thompson recognized the name immediately.

"Galen Morgan," she said aloud.

The evening nursing supervisor, who was giving report prior to going off duty, looked at her curiously. "You know him?"

"In a manner of speaking. What happened to him?"

"Hit by a car."

"Oh no."

"Where do you know him from? I know he was born here, but that was . . ."

". . . seven years ago," Willie finished for her. It didn't seem as if it could have been that long; she could still remember looking at him . . . at both of them . . . through the NICU window. "How bad is he?"

"He's in intensive care, just got out of surgery a little after ten."

"Critical?"

"I'm afraid so."

Willie wrote the word 'critical' next to Galen Morgan's name and drew a line beneath it. After report she would go up to ICU and see for herself.

Willie went directly to the ICU nurse's station, looking for answers.

The chart gave her some of them.

On arriving at the accident scene, the paramedics found the boy unconscious and unresponsive. Vital signs were taken, an esophageal airway was established, and an IV of Ringer's lactate was started. He was put into MAST pants due to suspected internal abdominal bleeding, and, after being moved onto a backboard with his head held in a neutral position, he was transported to the hospital emergency department.

In emergency he was evaluated by the emergency room physician who called for neurological and surgical consults. X rays were negative for skull or cervical fracture, but bilateral burr holes over the parieto-occipital and temporal regions confirmed a diagnosis of subdural hematoma. A CT head scan was scheduled prior to surgery. The scalp wound was cleaned and sutured. Bleeding from the left ear was investigated and found to be from the tympanic membrane which had been perforated.

The peritoneal tap was positive and a tentative secondary diagnosis of a ruptured spleen was arrived at. Urinalysis was negative for hematuria and urine volume was normal. Chest x-ray was normal. Blood was drawn for analysis and for type and crossmatch. A femoral stick was done to obtain arterial blood for blood gases.

Rather surprisingly, he had no broken bones, and the remainder of his injuries were minor contusions and abrasions which were cleaned using a betadine solution. Tetanus toxoid was given as a prophylactic measure.

Now Willie paused, looking at the 'coma' sheet, used in neurological evaluations to determine the level of coma. On arrival in emergency, Galen had opened his eyes only on painful stimuli and pupil reaction was sluggish bilaterally. He had made only incomprehensible sounds prior to the tracheotomy. He did not obey verbal commands to move his extremities, but had a flexion response to painful stimuli. His initial GCS score was eight out of fifteen. So there was hope, at least.

The next neurological evaluation—after he had a chance to recover from surgery and the anesthesia—would indicate whether he was improving or deteriorating. Then they would know whether the hope was justified.

If his coma deepened . . .

She looked across to where he lay.

"Oh, child," she said, and shook her head. It didn't seem right that he had to fight for his life twice.

A little later she went down to the basement to medical records to look for Galen's chart from 1979. The department was dark and deserted at this time of night, and as she moved among the long rows of shelves, she fought an impulse to hurry.

She found the boy's chart without difficulty, alongside that of his sister.

Kerri.

36

Willie frowned, straightening her shoulders and lifting her head to listen. A muffled noise, like a door being carefully closed, only . . .

For a moment she stood motionless, listening, but there was no other sound, and she turned from the shelf, the chart tucked under her arm, half-expecting to see a shape looming in the shadows.

But there was nothing there.

Chapter Six

Edana stood outside the emergency room entrance waiting for the cab.

It had rained while she was inside, and she thought at once of the blood on the pavement in front of the house, wondering if it had been washed away.

Blood and rain.

She shivered in the damp air, but made no move to go in out of the cold, preferring even a chill to the awful numbness that had plagued her since that instant in time . . .

If only it hadn't happened.

No, she told herself, don't think 'if only.' After Peter died, during the long weeks of her convalescence, her mind had offered countless alternative versions of the accident; if she had been driving, if they'd taken another road, if they'd left the party an hour earlier. Endless 'ifs' which only made it that much harder to accept what *had* happened.

If indeed she ever had accepted it.

Jeff didn't think she had, not yet. Or why, he would ask, did she insist on celebrating the twins' birthday a day late?

So she could mourn her dead husband alone?

Edana shook her head, bothered by the direction her thoughts were taking. To think of such things now would only drain her of energy needed for Galen . . . and Kerri.

Sitting in the back seat of the cab, Edana watched the dark houses, envying the peaceful sleep of those within. There were no other cars on the road, and the cab sped along the empty streets, passing beneath blinking traffic lights which stretched hypnotically into the distance.

The porch light was on.

She stood in the small circle of light and, her hands shaking, struggled to unlock the door. Behind her at the curb the cab idled, the driver waiting to see her safely in the house.

The key turned and the door cracked open.

Edana stepped into the hallway and closed the door behind her. Standing in the dark, she took a deep breath and then reached for the switch. Light flooded the room.

So it was real, then.

She was alone in the house. Alone as she had been in the weeks after her discharge from the hospital, before the twins were allowed to come home.

She could feel the emptiness of the rooms around her, the unnatural stillness of vacant space. Did she imagine it or was there already the musty smell of closed-up and abandoned rooms?

"You're crazy," she said to herself, and then walked quickly through the house, turning on lights, keeping back the dark.

In the kitchen she dumped cold hamburger clotted with hardened grease into the garbage, washed the skillet and wiped the stove clean. She scoured the sink, scrubbing futilely at a rust stain that had been there on the day they'd moved in.

And then stood in the middle of the room, staring out the window as the sky began to lighten behind the clouds.

It was Saturday morning.

SATURDAY

Chapter Seven

Kerri ran a comb through her hair, watching her reflection in the vanity mirror.

It was early and no one else was awake, but she'd looked out the window and seen the lights on in her house, and she knew that her mother was home.

With or without Galen.

From the hushed talk that passed between Mr. and Mrs. Bushard she guessed that Galen had been badly hurt. All last evening Mrs. Bushard had been giving her looks. And she'd gotten an extra dessert without even asking for it.

They were being very nice to her.

Kerri put the comb on the table and went to the window, pushing aside the curtain and pressing her face against the glass.

She wanted to go home.

Why hadn't her mother come for her?

Did her mother know?

Had Galen told?

Her warm breath fogged the window and she looked out through narrowed eyes, seeing, as from a distance, the expression on her brother's face.

He no longer wanted to play the games.

He no longer wanted to be like her.

Kerri tensed, remembering. The corners of her mouth turned down and her hands clenched into fists. She felt the stirring of rage as overhead the clouds darkened and lightning flashed.

It began to rain.

"Oh, Kerri."

Kerri breathed in the familiar clean smell of her mother's hair and stood still, allowing herself to be hugged. She could tell that her mother was near tears and waited to hear the news that her brother was dead.

"She was a little angel," Mrs. Bushard said, a quiver in her voice.

"Thank you for watching her for me."

"No trouble at all." That from Mr. Bushard, who sat puffing his pipe.

Kerri looked from one to the other and waited for someone to say something about Galen.

But no one did.

They walked home in silence. Kerri saw curtains fluttering in the houses along the way, and she knew that people were watching them.

Last night, long after the ambulance had taken Galen and her mother away, the neighbors had stood talking in the street.

She sensed their excitement, then and now.

Looking down, her dark hair hiding her face from curious eyes, she smiled.

Chapter Eight

"It's been acting up all night."

Calvin Hall raised one eyebrow. "Acting up?" he asked in as disdainful a manner as he could manage. He leaned back in the chair, surveying the computer console in front of him. The MEDLERT used in ICU was a sophisticated life support system, the cutting edge in medical technology. It had been designed to monitor every aspect of patient care, and was equipped with modules which could read and interpret cardiac rhythms, evaluate respiratory rates, trace brain wave activity, control drug and IV infusion rates, as well as providing continuous readings on blood pressure and body temperature.

It was, in his opinion, the ultimate in electronic monitoring. State of the art and then some.

A system like this one didn't 'act up.'

"What, exactly, did it do?"

The nurse looked at him blankly.

He tried again: "What's wrong with it?"

"If I knew what was wrong with it, I wouldn't need to call you," she said.

Calvin could feel his face stiffen with the effort of keeping his temper. It was too early for this: only a few minutes after seven, and he hadn't had his morning coffee yet. "I meant," he said carefully, "how is it . . . acting up?"

"All these lights keep going on and off." She pointed to the row of alarm indicators, none of which were lit.

"How about the audio alarms?" Each of the trouble lamps were backed up by a secondary audio alarm in case no one was watching the panel when an emergency condition occurred.

She shook her head. "Not a peep."

Calvin frowned, his eyes scanning the system function screen. Had someone accidentally disengaged the audio? It seemed unlikely; there were cross-checks throughout the entire system.

Hard to believe that anyone could access the operation commands—which were coded—accidentally or otherwise.

"Well?"

The nurse was watching him expectantly.

He sat down in front of the console, his fingers resting easily, familiarly, on the keyboard. He would ask the CPU to check its functions.

"This won't take long," he assured her.

He had only just logged on when the system blew.

The suspect audio alarms erupted in ear-splitting cadence, accompanied within seconds by the blare of the hospital intercom: "Code Blue, ICU. Code Blue in ICU."

Calvin stared in amazement at the flashing lights. Graph paper began to spew out from each of the sixteen thermal printers.

"Shit," he said, and started throwing switches, his first impulse to try and save the circuitry. Only after a

46

minute had passed did he look over the top of the console at the frenzied activity going on around him.

People were dying.

He swallowed hard, wanting to look away but unable to. A few feet away a doctor plunged a needle into a patient's chest, holding the barrel of the syringe like he would a knife, and grunting with the effort of it.

Calvin felt the blood leave his face.

The needle was withdrawn and tossed aside.

"Defibrillate," the doctor ordered.

One of the nurses positioned paddles on the patient's chest, then looked up. "Stand clear."

The rest of the code team moved away from the bed and watched as the body stiffened slightly as the electric current passed through it. Then they were back at it, surrounding the patient.

All that Calvin could see was the top of the man's head—wisps of white hair which clung damply to a scalp blotched with age.

Across the room, a second team worked on another patient.

The alarms stopped, finally.

Calvin worked diligently, concentrating on the computer and trying not to think of the two sheet-covered bodies now awaiting transfer to the morgue.

Keeping his eyes fixed to the screen, he tried not to hear the staff's speculations as to the cause of the deaths.

He had a horrid suspicion of his own.

Chapter Nine

"I'm sorry, Dr. Turner," the nurse said, handing her Galen Morgan's chart, "it's been a madhouse here."

"So I heard." News of the simultaneous deaths of two patients had circulated through the hospital within minutes, along with speculation as to the cause. "Has Dr. Abrahms been in this morning?"

"Not yet."

Megan glanced at her watch, mildly surprised. Abrahms had a reputation as being somewhat compulsive about his patients and had been known to stay at the hospital for several days straight—finding an empty bed and sleeping in his clothes—during the early critical stages of treatment.

"Has he called in?"

"No . . . at least I don't think so." The nurse sighed. "Actually, the Pope could have come through with Christ in tow and no one would have noticed, it's been that busy."

Megan smiled sympathetically and opened the chart to the medication log, verifying that the anticonvulsant was being given as ordered. She checked the morning lab results and then turned to the nursing progress notes.

The ICU nurse had documented Galen's vital signs and neurologic status at fifteen minute intervals throughout the night. Pupil reaction to light had improved, most probably in response to decreasing intracranial pressure. He had not, however, regained consciousness, nor had he demonstrated the restlessness which was indicative of "coming out" of a comatose state.

Blood pressure had decreased and stabilized, pulse was normal, but his temperature was up a full degree.

Writing quickly, Megan ordered acetaminophen as needed for fever, additional laboratory tests for glucose, electrolyte and blood urea nitrogen levels, and a portable chest x-ray.

She added an order for a physical therapist to assist the nurse in exercising the boy's joints and extremities so that . . . when . . . if . . . he awoke, his muscles would not have atrophied.

"Galen."

She stood at the bedside, her fingers encircling his wrist. His pulse was steady, his skin warm to the touch. She lifted his arm off the bed and let it go, watching as it fell limply.

He was so very still, she thought.

At the head of the bed a technician was attaching electrodes for an electroencephalogram.

"Look," the technician said, "he's dreaming."

Megan looked at the boy's face; beneath the eyelids, his eyes moved rapidly in a cyclic motion.

What dreams, she wondered, from that injured

49

brain.

Dr. Abrahms still hadn't turned up an hour later when she'd completed her rounds on the medical floor and returned to ICU.

"His exchange doesn't know where he is," the nurse informed her. "And his wife has been calling *us* looking for him."

"That's odd."

"Very . . . do you want me to have him call you when he does show up?"

Megan nodded. "And page me when Galen's mother comes to see him." Visiting hours in ICU were limited to ten minutes an hour between noon and ten at night, but when the patient was a child the rules were not strictly enforced.

"Will do."

As she started down the hall toward the doctor's lounge, they were paging Dr. Abrahms again.

Chapter Ten

Edana sat at the kitchen table, her hands cupped around a steaming mug of coffee.

Kerri had gone straight to her room when they'd gotten home, climbing the stairs without a backward glance. There hadn't been a sound out of her since.

Edana knew that she should talk to Kerri. Explain. But she despaired of being asked questions that she did not know the answers to. Children, she knew well, asked questions an adult never would.

Unless . . .

The police investigator had spoken with the neighbors and had left an official-looking card at the door. Written on the back of the card were two words: Please call.

Just that, nothing more.

She had known that they would want to talk to her. There had been a few questions last night . . . she half-remembered a policeman talking to her even before the ambulance had arrived . . . and then again in the quiet room . . . but no one had taken a statement. Had they?

No.

She took a sip of coffee. It was much stronger than she usually made it, and bitter, but she drank it anyway, and waited for the caffeine to have an effect. Her eyes itched from lack of sleep.

There was so much she had to do.

And there was nothing she could do.

Peter's desk took up one full corner of their bedroom. Old, massive, the wood dark and scarred, it was to her the very center of the house. Papers of any importance could be found in the deep drawers; birth certificates, their marriage certificate, financial records, insurance policies, the children's health records . . . all filed neatly away beside kindergarten drawings and the yellowed newspaper clippings she'd saved for all these years.

The photo albums were here, too.

In the middle drawer she found her address book, the same one she'd had since high school. The gold lettering had almost worn off the cover, and the pages had long since been filled.

Carefully, she turned to the M's.

There was Peter's name, written in ink in her then childish hand. Off to one side she had drawn a tiny heart.

She smiled.

He had teased her about the heart when he came across it after they were married, wanting to know when she'd been that certain of her feelings toward him.

"Our first kiss?" he'd ask, and kiss her.

"No."

"No?" More kisses, until she was breathless. "These are pretty great kisses," he would say solemnly. "Are you sure it wasn't our first kiss?"

"I'm sure."

"Second?"

"Not even close," she answered, pulling him back to her, eager for the taste of him.

It didn't take too much effort on her part to distract him, and the interrogation was forgotten for a while.

She never did tell him that she'd drawn the heart the same day she'd met him, long before the first date, seemingly ages before the first kiss.

John Morgan answered on the first ring.

"Hello?" His voice, so much like Peter's, came clearly across the line.

Her eyes tightly closed, Edana took a deep breath to steady her nerves.

"Hello?"

"Dad . . ." she said, and wondered how she could ever tell him.

"Edana, is that you?"

"It's me."

"Well," he said, "what do you know . . . I was just thinking about you and . . ." his voice faltered and she heard a sharp intake of breath. "Something's happened."

"Oh God," she said, and covered her mouth, trying to hold back the sob which rose in her throat.

"Edana, what is it? What's happened?"

"Galen." Her son's name came out as a whimper.

53

"Get hold of yourself," he said gently, "and tell me what happened to Galen."

She brushed away tears with the back of her hand. "He was hit by a car."

For a moment there was no response and she wondered if he'd heard, but she waited, not wanting to say those words again.

"Okay," he said, and she had the impression that he was talking to himself. "Okay. How bad . . ."

"He's at West Valley in ICU."

Another silence.

"Dad?"

"I'll be there on the next plane," he said. "Don't you worry, honey."

"Thank you."

"Just . . . hold on."

"I will," she promised.

She gathered clean sheets and towels from the linen closet and walked slowly toward Galen's room. Kerri's door was closed and she paused outside it, listening, but all she heard was a low-pitched hum, like static on a radio.

In Galen's room she stripped the bed and began making it up with the fresh sheets. His pajamas lay at the foot of the bed and she picked them up, holding the soft material to her face.

Outside, the wind blew the rain against the windows which rattled as if someone were trying to get in.

Chapter Eleven

Megan studied Galen Morgan's EEG, turning slowly through the folds of the graph paper, noting the presence of delta waves—slow waves with relatively high voltage—which supported the diagnosis of a lesion on the brain.

Beta waves predominated, however, indicating that the boy was in a sleep state; there were only short bursts of alpha waves.

Electroencephalography was, at best, an inexact science, since there had been reported cases of patients with severely injured brains producing "normal" exams. Conversely, patients without any neurologic or physical symptoms of brain disorders had yielded wildly abnormal readings.

What did it mean?

That they didn't know what was going on inside Galen Morgan's head.

Not very reassuring news for the boy's family.

She put the EEG into its folder and glanced at her watch. Edana Morgan had arrived at noon, according to the ICU nurse, and it was now twenty after.

With Abrahms still missing, it was her responsibil-

The ICU waiting room, through some master stroke of hospital planning, looked out across a cemetery.

Although it had been raining steadily all morning, a funeral was underway, the mourners gathered beneath a black canopy which buckled in the wind.

Edana Morgan stood silently at the window for a moment, watching, and then turned toward Megan. Her face was deathly pale, and Megan knew that she had been shocked by the sight of her son.

"This is much worse," Edana whispered, the words sounding as if they tore at her throat.

"Worse than what, Mrs. Morgan?"

"Then when he was born."

Megan had read the chart from 1979. "How do you mean?"

"He doesn't look," she said, "like he's going to live." She looked out the window again.

"He's been badly injured."

"His poor face . . ."

"He looks pretty bad right now," Megan acknowledged; the abrasions on his face and body had darkened to a purple-black color that made him resemble a ghoul from a George Romero movie, more dead than alive. "It's hard for you, I know, to see him that way."

Edana nodded, but kept her eyes fixed on the scene outside. "I thought, after all that's happened . . . I thought I was stronger than this."

"No one is ever prepared for accidents. But you got

through it when both of your children were in critical condition."

"It didn't hurt like this." Now she looked at Megan, her eyes shining with tears. "They were so tiny, they didn't seem real to me. I just looked at them through a window. I'd already lost so much, I don't remember feeling much of anything. I wanted to love them, but it just wasn't there." She took a deep breath. "But now . . . if he dies . . ."

"Youth is on his side," Megan said. "Children often survive injuries that would prove fatal to an adult. And we're doing all that we can."

Chapter Twelve

Kerri sat primly, her ankles crossed and her hands folded in her lap.

She'd been waiting in the hospital lobby for what seemed like a very long time. Much longer, she was certain, than any of the other children.

Looking out of the corners of her eyes, she watched them at play. They climbed over and under the furniture, hid behind the curtains, and took turns making the electric doors open. They pushed buttons on the pay phones, dug through an ashtray, and scattered magazines on the floor. They got drink after drink at the water fountain and collected water in their hands to carry dripping over to the potted plants.

They squirmed and whined and argued and screamed.

Kerri hated them.

She sniffed and looked away.

It was hard to believe that Galen could want to be like them. Playing silly, pointless games. Wasting time. Even worse, wasting energy.

Energy.

Kerri felt it building up inside her, a warm tingly feeling that increased in intensity the longer she went without using it. She could hear it, too, a humming sound that sometimes made it hard for her to listen to what people were saying.

Not that she cared; most of what people said wasn't worth listening to in the first place.

And she'd told them so.

A mind of her own, her mother said.

Willful, headstrong, stubborn and obstinate, said the others.

Galen had understood, even though he was less of all those things than she was.

But that was before.

The doors whooshed open behind her and a draft of cold air raised the hair on her arms.

"Hello."

Kerri shifted her eyes. There were two of them; one a girl about her own age, the other a boy at least three years younger. They stood across from her, a few feet away.

She nodded but did not answer.

"Who you waiting for?" the girl asked, slurring the words.

Kerri looked closely at the girl's face. It was a broad face, familiar somehow, the eyes slanted, the nose flattened and scabbed at the nostrils. The girl's cheeks were red, like she'd been out in the cold.

The boy tugged at the girl's hand.

"Come on, Debbie," he urged, trying to pull her away, but she was much bigger and she was not going.

"Who you waiting for?" she said again, her tongue

59

twisting around the words as if it were painful to talk.

Then Kerri knew.

There were two of them at school. Two kids in the special classes who looked just like this girl.

Mongoloids, the other kids called them, hooting with laughter and pulled the corners of their eyes up, making fun when the teachers weren't looking.

Sometimes the kids from special classes came to assembly, but when they did, the other kids would pinch them and poke them, and call them names.

Retard.

Dummy.

Kerri had never taken part, but then, she never took part in any of their games.

She looked from the girl to the boy, who was still tugging insistently, and uselessly, on the girl's arm.

When he noticed that she was now watching him, he tensed, his eyes opening wide.

"Debbie," he pleaded, "come on."

So he's afraid, Kerri thought.

"My mother," Kerri finally said. "I'm waiting for my mother."

The girl's face split in a smile and she nodded. "Me too," she said, and then ambled off. The boy, after a quick glance over his shoulder, guided the girl over to a far corner of the room, well away from the other children.

He needn't have feared; Kerri understood about Debbie. She knew about being different.

Chapter Thirteen

Looking out the small rectangle that the airline tried to pass off as a window, John Morgan frowned. Below, sprawled as far as the eye could see, was Los Angeles. Los Angeles, to his way of thinking, was a wasteland. Never mind that the streets were teeming with life; it was not a good place to live. And Orange County? More of the same.

He had never understood why Peter had chosen to leave Iowa and live among this madness.

Nor, after Peter died, why Edana had refused his offer to come back with him to the farm.

At least she brought the twins to visit every summer.

The plane was descending, slowing, and he kept a careful eye on the flaps on the wing. How could a little thing like that slow down a big plane like this? Didn't seem that it could, and maybe it wouldn't.

Just in case, he cinched his seat belt a little tighter.

Flying, he thought, was for the birds.

Then the wheels touched down and the nose came down, and the brakes were on.

He had survived his third flight in sixty-one years.

"Welcome to Los Angeles," the stewardess said.

Los Angeles welcomed him by raining all over him while he waited for a shuttle bus to take him into Orange County. Around him people scurried, lugging bags and in some cases leading them on a leash like a pet dog.

Only in L.A., he was sure.

His own bag, a battered brown case he'd had before Peter was born, sat at his feet, a faded baggage tag—from 1979—below the new one.

He didn't know why he hadn't thrown the first tag away. Hadn't got around to it, he supposed.

Time passed and you forgot, at least some things.

Some things were always with you.

Like Mary crying at their son's grave, and then dying herself only six months later.

And now Galen.

He felt moisture at his eyes and wiped at them with one trembling hand.

"Lot of good you're going to do, old man," he said to himself, and turned his face into the rain.

The LAX-Orange County Express pulled up and John situated himself in the seat behind the driver, intending to keep a close eye on things. Never hurt to let them know they were being watched.

Waiting for the other passengers to finish boarding, he took a last look at the airport.

LAX. What the hell was the X for? Any fool knew that international was abbreviated int-apostrophe-l.

Uppity, the whole damn city.

Crossing his arms across his chest, he settled back

as the shuttle finally pulled away from the curb.

The sound of the motor lulled him into a half-sleep.

Peter, racing down the dirt road toward him as he drove the John Deere in from the fields.

A small sturdy boy with hair as golden as wheat at harvest, his bare feet raising dust in the still afternoon air.

"Dad . . . Dad." Running alongside.

Mary's blue eyes, dark and clear, and showing the intelligence behind them.

"What is it, boy?"

Ruffling a hand through that sweat-dampened hair.

"Kittens, we've got kittens."

As if that was a surprise, as if every spring and fall the mamma cat didn't have a new litter. You could hardly walk across the yard without tripping over a cat.

But he asked: "How many?"

"Four." Peter held up a grubby hand, four fingers splayed wide.

"Figures."

"There's a black one," Peter said excitedly, "and a yellow, and two mixed."

"Yup . . . sounds about right."

"Mom says," he panted, "that I can name 'em."

"Don't see why not." John reached down, leaning from the height of the tractor seat, and pulled his son up into the cab.

"Can I drive?"

63

"Don't see why not." He took his big hands off the wheel and eased up on the accelerator. Peter held on tight, holding the wheel steady.

He must have been six that year.

John blinked and wiped at his eyes, and then his face. He took a deep breath and cleared his throat.

He noticed the driver watching him in the rear-view mirror.

It didn't bother him, though; he was entitled to his tears and he lifted his chin with pride. The driver looked away.

He searched the signs along the freeway for a clue as to where they were. Off-ramps for Beach Boulevard, Brookhurst, LaPalma and Euclid.

As certain as he had been that he'd never forget the first trip out here, he apparently had. None of the street names meant anything to him.

But then he saw the unmistakable shape of that runt Alpine mountain, rising incongruously on the right.

Disneyland.

Maybe he'd take the kids . . . when Galen was better.

He handed a slip of paper with Edana's address on it to the cab driver and sat back in the seat, stretching his legs. After the plane and the shuttle, it was good to be in a real live car again.

The cab darted into traffic and pulled an illegal U-turn. Horns sounded from every direction; the driver was oblivious to it all.

"You from New York?" John asked, holding onto the back of the seat.

"Newport."

"Rhode Island?"

"Beach."

The driver accelerated through a red light.

Better not to watch, John decided.

John pulled the bag from the back seat of the cab and then dug into his pocket for the fare.

It was just starting to get dark, a little after five, California time, and lights shone in the windows of the houses along the street.

Only the porch light was on at Edana's house; she was probably still at the hospital.

For a moment he stood at the curb, remembering the last time he was here, and then he pulled out his keys. Edana had given him a key—Peter's key—back in '79.

"In case," she'd said, pressing it into his hand.

Picking up his bag, he walked slowly toward the house.

Chapter Fourteen

"You can use this room," the nurse said, holding the door open and standing aside.

"Thank you." Matt Kennedy nodded at the nurse and then looked at the boy's mother. "This won't take long," he said.

For a minute he pretended to leaf through his notes, timing his glances for when she was looking away. An attractive woman in spite of her obvious distress. Her face, though pale and drawn, was highlighted by wide-set blue eyes with the darkest fringe of lashes he'd ever seen.

She turned her gaze to his, catching him watching.

"I was going to call for an appointment."

He smiled, hoping to put her at ease. People were always defensive when they talked to him, even now that he was no longer in uniform.

"I figured you'd be here seeing your son," he explained. "How is he, by the way?"

Pain flashed in her eyes. "Alive, so far."

"This is a good hospital." For some reason he wanted to reassure her. "One of the best."

"Yes, I know."

"I'm sure . . ." he glanced down at the police reports to find the boy's name.

"Galen," she supplied.

". . . Galen . . . will be all right." As soon as the words were out of his mouth he realized how empty they sounded, but she smiled faintly.

"Thank you."

He couldn't think of an adequate response to that; 'you're welcome' seemed out of line. Instead he shuffled through the reports, aware now that she was watching him.

"I'm sorry," she said. "I didn't catch your name?"

"Matthew Kennedy." Out of habit he extended his hand.

"Edana Morgan."

Her hand disappeared into his, and he had to remind himself to let go.

"Mrs. Morgan," he said, "I understand you witnessed your son's accident."

"Yes."

"Can you tell me what you saw? From just before the accident."

She blinked and seemed to pull back, then looked down at her hands which she held almost as if in prayer.

He noticed that she still wore her wedding ring, and wondered how long ago her husband had died. 'Deceased' was all it said in the reports.

"Galen had gone outside," she said, measuring her words. "He walked down the sidewalk to the curb . . ."

"Excuse me, what time was this, do you have any idea?"

"Yes, it was just after five, maybe two or three minutes. I was in the kitchen fixing dinner, and I'd just looked at the clock when I heard his voice from upstairs."

"What did he say?"

She looked up at him. Tears glistened in her eyes.

"He said 'no'."

He couldn't look away from her, could not make himself write the word.

"Then what happened?"

"I heard him running down the stairs . . . I went to see . . . what was wrong . . . and I saw him run out of the house."

"Go on."

"He went to the curb and stopped there." Again she hesitated, and looked away from him. Her hands were open, now, palms up on her lap, and she studied them as if looking for answers.

Matt wanted to take her hand into his and make her look at him again. He wanted her to see the sympathy in his eyes. He wanted her to know . . . what?

That he suspected that her son had attempted suicide?

"Then," she said, her voice oddly lifeless, "he turned and yelled 'no' again . . . and he stepped off the curb, right in front of the car."

Matt handed her a styrofoam cup full of coffee and sat down opposite her.

"I'm sorry," she said.

"Don't be . . . I know this must be very hard for

68

you." He regarded her seriously.

Again, a hint of a smile.

Trite. Why was everything he said so damned trite?

They sat for a while in silence.

She did not, thank God, ask him what he thought about what had happened to her son. And he did not ask her what she thought; some things were better left unsaid.

He wrote his home phone number on the back of his card and handed it to her.

"If you can't reach me at the station," he said, feeling the warmth begin to rise in his face.

"Thank you."

"In case you have any questions about the investigation." The explanation, if that's what it was, sounded awkward, but what else could he say?

He watched her walk down the hall toward ICU.

There had been a five car pile-up on the freeway and the emergency room was swarming when he walked through on his way out.

It had been some time since he'd last worked patrol, but he recognized the stench of burned flesh and caught a glimpse of a smoke-darkened face.

Life in the city, he thought.

Chapter Fifteen

"Calvin, what are you doing here?"

Calvin looked up from the computer console. One of the nurses, he didn't know her name, was smiling—or leering—at him. "I think it's fairly evident that I'm working."

"But you never work nights. And Saturday nights . . . isn't this cutting into your social life?"

"I don't have time for a social life."

"That's too bad," she said, stretching her plump arms up in a poorly conceived attempt at titillation. Her breasts, he noticed, sagged woefully.

"Yes, well, life is full of disappointments." He turned his attention back to the computer.

"You'd be surprised."

He ignored the remark and after a few minutes of pretending that she had business there, the nurse wandered off.

Calvin regarded the computer.

He was at a loss. He had been able to think of nothing else all day. And nothing he thought of brought him closer to a conclusion about what had gone wrong.

He hadn't a clue.

Well, maybe one clue.

It might have been a power surge.

But if it was, it had originated somewhere here in ICU. A machine malfunctioning, or . . .

Reddy Kilowatt committing hari-kari in the wires?

His eyes wandered around the room.

Machines everywhere.

He would have to check every one of them.

Chapter Sixteen

"Megan, give us a hand?"

Megan turned to see Dave Levine and a team of nurses pushing a gurney toward the rear elevators.

Catching up to them, she saw that the patient was swathed in sterile dressings.

"Burn victim," David said. "Hold this." He handed her a syringe, the needle embedded in the gasket of the stop cock which allowed the medication to be infused via the IV line.

They all piled into the elevator and now Megan could smell the burned flesh.

Dave leaned over the gurney as well as he could, given his height and girth, so the patient could see him. "You'll be in the air in five minutes, and at UCI in ten."

Then he looked at Megan and frowned.

The heliport was located on the roof of the building and when the elevator doors opened into the holding area they could see the helicopter touching down.

Seconds later the air ambulance medics were running toward them, heads kept low under the path of the copter blades.

Megan and Dave went alongside the gurney, standing by as the patient was loaded on board.

"Hang tough," Dave yelled over the noise.

Megan thought she saw the patient's mouth move, but if he spoke, it was lost in the wind.

"Wait a minute," Dave shouted, and took the syringe, injecting an additional 2 cc's of morphine into the patient's vein. "That way it won't hurt so damn much."

Then they ran back to the shelter and turned to watch the helicopter lift off.

It had just cleared the building and hospital grounds when they saw something white flash in the cockpit, and it tilted to the left, flying almost on its side, before the rotor blades stopped and it dropped silently from the sky, exploding on impact.

SUNDAY

Chapter Seventeen

At midnight, finally, the hospital was quiet again.

Looking into the night, Rita could see the flashing lights and flares that marked off the scene of the helicopter crash, but the sirens had long since faded.

No one had survived.

Turning from the window, she filled the wash basin with lukewarm water and then carried it across to the cabinet next to Galen Morgan's bed. From her pocket she took a small plastic package of liquid Castile soap which she emptied into the stainless steel bowl.

He'd had a bath on the day shift, according to the progress notes, but Rita knew how superficially things were done by the day nurses, with doctors interrupting them every five minutes.

It was very important that the boy be clean.

As she drew the curtain around the bed she noticed a brownish stain near the hem and she made a mental note to call housekeeping. It might take a little 'convincing'—there was only one housekeeper on at night and he was reluctant to do much of anything— but the curtain would be changed . . . and soon.

Then, almost reverently, she turned to the boy.

Galen lay perfectly still.

Rita wrung out the washcloth and with infinite care, she began his bath.

There were, as she had expected, little flecks of dried blood on his left arm from where they'd drawn the six p.m. lab tests, and she lathered the area thoroughly. The puncture wound itself, she noted, was slightly reddened; she would have to watch it carefully for any signs of infection.

She shook her head in irritation. "Damn lab techs," she said.

A minute later she was ready to add doctors to the list; the cutdown above his left ankle was definitely puffy and inflamed.

Didn't they know how critical it was that all of his body's energies be focused onto healing his brain? A secondary infection in his blood—caused by someone's carelessness or downright incompetence—might be more than his system could handle.

He was only a little boy.

Well, her notes on the progress report would include a scathing remark or two about sterile procedures and infection control.

What was the doctor's creed; 'do no harm'?

Sighing, she washed around the cutdown site and then applied a betadine dressing.

When the left side was done she drew the sheet back over him and carried the basin to the other side of the bed. Placing the basin on top of the set-up tray, she saw the wrappings from an arterial blood gas kit.

They'd stuck him again.

Pulling the sheet and his gown aside, she looked for the wound in his groin, knowing respiratory's proclivity for femoral sticks.

It didn't take much to find it; the area was swollen and discolored beneath the skin where blood had leaked from the artery after the needle was removed. Procedure dictated that *they* were to apply pressure over the artery for five full minutes after removing the needle to prevent this type of thing. Obviously none of *them* could tell time.

Then her eyes were drawn to something else, something it took her a few seconds to comprehend.

Several of the connector cables to the various monitors were wound around Galen's right arm.

His fingers were entwined among the wires.

Her eyes shifted to his face.

Eyes closed, mouth opened slightly, he was, she thought, dead to the world.

He had not shown even the smallest sign of wakening.

He was, in fact, being sedated.

Yet clearly the only way for his arm to have gotten tangled in the cables was for him to have done it himself. Lifting his arm off the bed and then circling it beneath and around the lines.

So what was going on?

It took her twenty minutes to free his arm from its electric web.

Never once, during that time, did the boy move.

Chapter Eighteen

"It'll make you feel better," John Morgan said, pouring wine into his daughter-in-law's glass.

Sitting in the living room in a small circle of light cast by a single lamp, he studied her for signs of how she was holding up. She looked tired, certainly, but there was a strength in her face that he hadn't noticed before.

Edana had arrived home just after eleven and he'd gone out to help her with Kerri who'd fallen asleep in the back seat of the car. For a moment, following her up the stairs with his granddaughter in his arms, it had been like stepping into his past, and he was glad that he didn't have to say anything just then, what with the lump in his throat.

After settling Kerri for the night, they'd come down to talk.

The wine, he hoped, would make it easier for both of them.

"I went a little crazy," Edana said softly, looking into her glass.

"Understandable."

"Did I ever tell you . . . I went to see the car?"

He knew at once that this was about Peter. "No, you never did."

"There were some papers the insurance man needed . . . in the glove compartment."

John frowned and took a sip of wine. It seemed to him that any papers regarding insurance that Peter might have kept in the car ought to have been duplicated elsewhere—like in the insurance man's files. But that was neither here nor there, so he kept his peace.

"I'd never been to a wrecking yard before," she said.

"I wouldn't expect that you had."

She glanced his way and he could see it in her eyes, that no matter how many years had passed, nor how many ever would, this was hurting her. A raw and painful memory.

He saw just as clearly that she had to talk about it.

"It didn't even look like a car."

There had been a picture in the newspaper, when he and Mary had come out to see if there was anything they could do. Mary kept all the clippings but he hadn't wanted to see. Later he'd come across them, and wished he hadn't.

Edana was right; it looked nothing like a car.

"The firemen had to pry the top of the car off to get him out."

One of the clippings said it took them over an hour; John wondered if she knew.

"The steering wheel was pushed almost into the back seat. It . . . cracked on impact . . ."

Now he had to look away, thinking of Peter on that

81

spring day, sitting between him and the steering wheel of the tractor. Imagining an impact strong enough to crack hard plastic. What it must do to a man's chest.

"There was . . ."

Knowing what was coming, he met her eyes.

". . . dried blood . . . all over the place."

Their eyes held for a long moment.

"I think he died quickly," she said. "Before help came. He died beside me, Dad, without my knowing."

Something told him to stay quiet, and let her finish.

"They took me away and I never got a chance to say goodbye, and I never got a chance to tell him how much I loved him."

He nodded, understanding. Peter had been buried before Edana was told of his death; for a while there was doubt that she would survive the dual shock of her injuries and the birth of the twins. The doctors said it might be weeks before she was strong enough to be told.

At the time it had seemed like the right thing to do. To tell her now that Peter knew how much she loved him would be missing the point; she was entitled to mourn her husband in her own way. She'd been denied so much by circumstance . . .

"I went a little crazy when he died," she said. "I don't think I can go through it again."

"Lord love you," he said, and swallowed hard, knowing that there was not a thing in his power to do that would make a whit of difference where little

Galen was concerned.

Except maybe pray.

He reached across and took her hand. "Whatever happens . . . you won't be alone."

Chapter Nineteen

Kerri waited until she was certain that they were asleep, well past the time she'd heard their footsteps on the stairs and their hushed whispers of good night. Her mother, she knew, was a light sleeper but having had so little rest since Friday, Kerri thought she would sleep deeply if not well.

Grandfather snored.

Slipping the covers aside, Kerri sat on the edge of the bed looking at the window and contemplated what she might do.

She never had without Galen.

He had been the one who started it all.

When they were little, mother always said that the odd things that happened—lights going on and off in empty rooms, the television turning on in the middle of the night, a succession of blenders whose motors burned out on first use—were all a result of bad wiring in the house.

Other things, like the car battery exploding on their first day of school and fire alarms going off in store after store when she took them shopping, she called "coincidences."

Galen had been first to realize that it was them. They were doing these things.

And other people weren't able to.

He had shown her by making the record player run in reverse, spinning faster and faster until the sound was nothing but a loud and senseless noise. Then, going to a window, he had made first one car and then another stall in the street.

She could still remember the smile on his face when he turned to look at her.

"Try it, Kerri," he said.

It was easy.

She rang the doorbells of every house on the block, and laughed in delight at the perplexed faces of the neighbors as door after door opened . . . and no one was there.

She smiled, remembering.

"Just for fun," Galen said, and that was what it had been. For a while.

Now she walked silently over to the window and looked out on the deserted street. The rain had softened to a mist which made rainbow halos around the streetlights.

Kerri touched the glass and warmed it, feeling the power in her fingertips.

What first, she thought.

Outside the streetlights began to flicker and she watched dispassionately as the one nearest the house went dark.

Not good enough.

In rapid succession, three of the globes exploded,

showering blue-white sparks onto the wet pavement as fragments of glass whistled through the air.

She turned her gaze toward the more distant lights.

Alternating from one side of the street to the other, the streetlights disintegrated in a flurry of white flashes.

It was beautiful.

Chapter Twenty

"Hot damn."

Curtis did not believe how good his luck was going. Since switching to the night shift, it had been one slick move after the other. He was just falling into clover. It was knee deep and getting higher.

Life was good.

Whistling softly, he pushed open the door to the fire stairs and half-danced over to the rail.

A stewardess, and hallelujah.

Stacked, packed and soon to be racked.

Amazing how many women, when they saw him in his hospital greens, took him to be an intern. Doctor-to-be. Wealthy, as it were, in waiting.

Nobody'd told him when he applied for a job as an orderly about the fringe benefits.

He smiled and dug into his pockets for a smoke.

If it kept up this way, he might have to consider selling franchises.

Doctor Love, he'd call them.

It was the perfect scam.

And he, Curtis Lee Frenz, ("Rhymes with Benz," he'd say, and watch their little eyes glitter with Car

Lust) had thought of it all on his own.

His mama had raised a genius.

"Damn, Curtis," he said, an unlit cigarette dangling from his mouth, "you cool."

It was all in the approach. And knowing opportunity when it was staring you in the face.

The first one had been a meter maid with a chest cold. Judging by the size of her chest, the cold must have been hard put to cover the territory.

He'd opened the door of one of the back E.R. examining rooms, thinking that it was empty and hoping to catch a nap.

When he saw her, wrapped in only a thin sheet, his heart—among other things—gave a leap.

"Excuse me," he said and started backing out.

"Oh doctor," the meter maid said, dropping the sheet down to her waist. "I've been waiting so long."

He looked behind him, checking to see if anyone was in the hall, but there was no one in sight.

Then he closed the door.

Never let it be said that a woman waited for him and went unrewarded.

He had since refined his technique.

All he had to do was put those little booties the surgeons wore over his shoes, sling a stethoscope around his neck, and mess up his hair and voila! A doctor.

He also refrained from dispensing his special brand of medical care on the hospital premises. One encounter spent looking over his shoulder, waiting for the door to open and a nurse to come in (armed, no doubt, with a six-inch needle) was more than enough for him.

No, as they always said, discretion was the better part of . . . well, the better part of something, anyway.

As it happened, the solution proved to be a natural outgrowth of working nights.

Closing his eyes, he remembered the second time . . . and the second lady.

It was nearing seven a.m. and time to go off duty, and he'd walked along the back hall behind E.R., not really expecting to strike gold twice.

She was pulling her sweater over her head when he opened the door.

And he'd bless women's liberation for their bra-burning rites to the end of his days.

"Oh, doctor." She smiled and pulled the sweater down very slooowwly.

"Hi," he said; that was before he'd developed his line.

Her eyes took in the booties and he knew she understood the significance of them by the way her pink tongue licked the corners of her lips.

"Are you just getting off?"

"Close to it," he said.

"You were on all night?"

Mouth dry, he nodded.

"Would you like something to eat?"

He had heard that same question from his mama, had to be a million times, but he knew that this time the menu was something else again.

"Sure."

"My place?"

"Absolutely."

He found out later that she taught English to fifth graders; she was particularly good at keeping parts from dangling.

So it was that he had breakfasted with a legion of women, all of whom had an eye on his M.D.

As long as he worked nights, there was no question of him having to take them out on the town, and all of them were more than willing to demonstrate their domestic and other skills. Giving aid and comfort to a man of medicine was their small contribution to improving the quality of life.

In fact one of them, an aspiring actress with an insatiable appetite for retakes, had improved his life to the point that he considered foregoing all the rest.

But he'd come to his senses in time, knowing that it wouldn't take even her too long to figure out that the reason he always arrived at her apartment in a cab was because he drove a multi-colored 1963 Ford Falcon with bald tires and a front shimmy that'd set her capped teeth to rattling.

Nope, it was best to hit and run.

Always leave 'em wanting just a little more.

He decided to take the stairs on down to the basement and shoot the breeze for a while with whoever was working in central service before taking his three a.m. break.

His footsteps echoed in the stairwell.

Outside the air had become opaque as the mist condensed into a swirling fog.

He wet his fingers and touched his pelvis.

"Tsss," he said to the fog, "you want steam, I'll give you steam. This man is hot!"

Then he pushed the door open into the basement landing, his eyes taking in the bundle of sheets half hidden under a wall storage unit.

Except sheets didn't have hair.

And sheets didn't bleed all over the floor.

And sheets weren't looking at him with glazed, dead eyes.

"Oh, man," he said.

It was Dr. Abrahms and he was stone cold.

Chapter Twenty-one

"Have you heard?" Willie Thompson asked.

Megan looked up from Galen Morgan's chart and nodded. Word of Dr. Abrahms' death had circulated quickly. "Are the police still here?"

"The police, administration, the coroner. I imagine they'll be a while yet; it isn't every day that a prominent neurosurgeon gets killed in a hospital basement." She pulled up a chair and sat down.

"Do they know that for sure? He was killed there?"

"They're not saying, at least not to a lowly nursing supervisor, but I know a little about forensics and a lot about the human body, and with all that blood . . ."

"Of course, you're right."

"Now, who would want to do such a thing, that I wouldn't know."

Megan closed the chart. "It's hard to imagine . . . he was a good man."

"The only neurosurgeon I ever met who didn't think he walked on water," Willie said, and motioned toward the chart. "How's his patient, by the way."

"Better. It looks as if he's trying to breathe on his own; we may be able to start weaning him off the respirator any time now."

"That is wonderful news."

Megan regarded Willie curiously, a little surprised at the intensity of emotion in the supervisor's voice.

As a supervisor, and particularly working nights, Willie would have little patient contact. Yet it was obvious, by both what she said and the way she said it, that Galen meant something to her.

And Willie wasn't the only one who felt that way about the boy.

When Megan arrived in ICU an hour before, Rita Cortez had been drawing Galen's blood for the morning labs while the technician stood by watching.

Rita refused to let the tech do his job, because, Megan heard her say, "You're hurting him."

Chapter Twenty-two

John Morgan stood on the porch, the newspaper that he'd come out to get forgotten in his hand, and looked with amazement at what was left of the streetlights. Broken glass littered the pavement but nowhere was there a sign of whatever had been used to break it.

Had someone shot the lights out?

"Dad?"

He turned to see Edana pushing open the screen door.

"What is it?"

"Some fool held open season on the light poles."

"Oh God," she said, and pulled her robe tighter around her.

She looks better this morning, he thought, watching as she stepped off the porch for a better view of the street. Her dark hair had been swept up off her slender neck into an old-fashioned bun, the way she'd worn it on her wedding day. A fine looking woman, his son's wife.

"What a mess."

"It is that."

94

"This type of thing is always happening around here."

"Well," he said mildly, "it wouldn't happen back home."

She gave him a look. "You don't even have street-lights back home."

"But if we did . . ."

The smile on her face gladdened his heart.

He made breakfast, happy, for a change, to be cooking for other than just himself. A skillet didn't look right with only one egg in it.

Kerri, looking pale and a little drawn, picked at her food for a few minutes and then excused herself.

"I'm sorry, Dad. She never eats much when she's upset."

He passed it off with a wave of his hand. "She's entitled."

Edana sighed. "I know this is hard on her. She's been so quiet lately. They won't let her in to see Galen . . . of course, I understand why . . . but I think it's made it worse for her. What I mean is . . . I'm sure she imagines he's much worse than he really is."

John hesitated, feeling the dread build inside him. It was time, he knew, to confront his own imagination about Galen's injuries.

"Edana . . . tell *me* about Galen."

She looked surprised for a moment but then nodded. "We haven't really talked about him, have we?"

"No."

"It's odd . . . I've told the story so many times . . .

to doctors, nurses, even the police . . . that it just seems to me that everyone should *know*."

"It wasn't just you," he said. "I guess I've always thought that ignorance is bliss . . . part of me doesn't want to know. When you called the other day, I had questions, thousands of questions, that I couldn't bring myself to ask. It's hard to say the words . . . I keep thinking about Peter . . ."

"So do I."

"But . . . time has come."

"All right," she said and then, her voice barely audible, she told him about Peter's son.

"Yes?"

A young man about Edana's age stood on the porch.

"Ah, good morning. Is Edana here?"

John grunted. "Who are you?"

"A friend of hers, Jeff Garrett."

John looked him up and down. Maybe an inch under six feet tall, slim, dark hair, gray eyes so pale they were almost colorless. Neatly dressed in chinos and a plaid wool shirt. Good looking, John supposed.

"A friend?"

"Yes sir . . . we're in nursing school together."

"You're going to be a nurse?"

A quick smile. "Yes, sir, I am. Is Edana here?"

He had just about decided to send Garrett packing when Edana came up behind him.

"Jeff!"

Then he moved aside and watched as Edana allowed herself to be embraced by her friend, going into his arms like she belonged there. Like she was safe there.

They stood that way for what seemed to be a long time.

Their voices carried into the kitchen where he was drying the breakfast dishes.

He wasn't exactly trying to eavesdrop, but neither was he inclined to move out of hearing distance.

"Edana . . . why didn't you call me?"

"Every time I thought about it, it was the middle of the night."

Garrett's voice softened. "I wouldn't mind; that's what friends are for."

John snorted.

"I know, and you've been a good friend to me. But I can't always cry on your shoulder."

"You can if you need to . . ."

"I just . . . I needed to stay in control."

"What do you mean?"

"It would have been so easy for me to call and let you come take over for me. To abdicate . . . to give in to it and just be carried along."

"But something like this," Garrett protested, "you shouldn't have been alone . . ."

"I needed to be alone for a while."

"You're okay then?"

"I am . . . and I'm also glad you came."

Silence.

John busied himself at the sink, turning the water on and whistling, anything to keep from hearing the quiet in the next room.

"Dad?"

John turned, hoping that his smile looked more

natural than it felt.

"Jeff has volunteered to stay here with Kerri so you can come to the hospital with me and see Galen."

Garrett stood behind Edana in the doorway, one hand on her shoulder. John searched his daughter-in-law's face for what Mary had always called "high color," the flush that a woman got when she was near a man she cared for.

He was relieved that he didn't find it.

"Well," he said, and smiled harder. "I'd best get my jacket."

He didn't ask her about Garrett, but he studied her as she drove.

Seven years was a long time to be alone.

Chapter Twenty-three

"Galen, it's Mama," Edana whispered in her son's ear and moved back, watching his face for any reaction. Had his eyelashes fluttered or was it wishful thinking?

"He's doing better today," the nurse said.

Edana looked up. "Is he?"

"His vital signs are stable and there've been no new signs of intracranial bleeding."

"Is he going to have another brain scan?"

The nurse nodded. "Tomorrow morning, first thing."

"And another EEG?"

"It hasn't been ordered yet, I mean, I suppose you heard."

"Heard?" Edana felt the first tingling of alarm. "About what?"

"Dr. Abrahms."

"No, I haven't." She could see by the nurse's expression that whatever it was, it wasn't good.

"He's dead."

For a moment she thought she had misheard, but the word, which had haunted her ever since the accident, would not go away. "Dead?"

"I'm sorry, Mrs. Morgan," the nurse said, obviously flustered, "I thought someone had told you . . . since he was your son's doctor."

Her mind raced with confusion. The only thing she could think of was that there'd been an accident; a dreadful irony for a man whose skill had saved lives to lose his own to chance. "But . . . what happened?"

"The police think he was murdered."

"What?" Several of the other nurses were looking in their direction and she made an effort to lower her voice. "When?"

"I don't think they know yet, but . . . he'd been missing since early Saturday morning."

Edana stared at her blankly. "I didn't know. I . . . what about Galen?"

"Dr. Stafford will be taking over," the nurse said.

"Who?"

"Dr. Benjamin Stafford."

She looked from the nurse to her son, and thought, for a second, that his mouth had moved as if to speak.

"He's an excellent doctor," the nurse said.

Edana stood near the window which faced the cemetery, and tried to make sense of something she was certain there was no sense to.

John had gone in to be with Galen and she was the only one in the room; Sunday morning was apparently not a prime time for visiting.

She watched a woman walk slowly along a path which wound among the neatly-tended rows of graves. Flowers in hand, the woman stopped at intervals, looking around her as if uncertain where she was.

Edana knew the feeling.

According to a police spokesman, Dr. Abrahms had, "with a high degree of probability," been killed on the hospital grounds. Time of death was being estimated as being between the hours of midnight and six a.m. Saturday morning.

She'd left the hospital shortly after midnight that night.

Was he dead even as she'd stood waiting in the cold for the taxi?

Did he die even as she prayed for him to save Galen's life?

It was dreadful to think that in having come in to help her child he had placed his own life in jeopardy.

Dreadful to wonder whether if by being in this one place at that one specific time he had stumbled into a madman's fantasy, and died as a result of it.

Was the killer still around?

She shivered.

Across the way, the woman placed the flowers on a grave and then stood, her head bowed.

Too late, Edana thought. Too late.

Chapter Twenty-four

"What," Matt Kennedy asked himself, "am I doing here?"

It was a nice neighborhood, the houses all well tended, lawns a little overgrown because of the spate of rain they'd had. Quiet, he thought, even for a Sunday.

Edana Morgan lived in an old two-story house, painted white, and set just a little further back from the road than the others on the street. A small garage, separate from the house, was off to the left.

A dark blue Porsche was parked in the driveway.

He knew it wasn't her Porsche; what would a woman with two kids do with a racy little job like that? Company?

He didn't want to intrude.

Maybe he'd better come back another time.

What was he doing here anyway?

He reached for the car key and then stopped, hand in mid-air. The front door to her house opened and a young girl came out.

The daughter . . . what was her name?

As he watched, the girl, dark-haired like her

mother, moved across the porch and stood looking, he thought, at the trees along the street. From this distance it was hard to see her expression, but there was an attitude about her of . . . exultation?

Curious, he followed her gaze.

At first all he saw were the trees. Overhead, rays of sunlight streamed down between thinning clouds and blue sky peeked through for the first time in days.

Then he noticed the streetlights.

When he looked back at the porch, the girl had disappeared.

He was surprised when a man answered the door. Surprised and . . . what? Something more, he knew.

The guy looked like the type to drive a Porsche. "Yes?"

Out of habit, or maybe to ease his own discomfort, he flashed his badge. "Is Mrs. Morgan in?"

"She's at the hospital."

Of course, he thought. "When do you expect her?"

"I couldn't say."

Matt studied the man's face. He had no business asking, but he couldn't stop himself: "And you are . . ."

A quick smile. "A friend."

Matt smiled back, the hard policeman's smile that never reached his eyes. "Would you mind," he said, digging into a pocket for one of his cards, "asking Mrs. Morgan to give me a call?"

"At her convenience?"

"What?"

"Is it urgent or can it wait?"

He hesitated. "At her earliest convenience." He held the card out.

The screen door opened and the *friend* reached for the card.

"Wait a minute," Matt said, and cupping the card in his palm, quickly wrote his home phone number on the back. "If she can't reach me at work."

"This is police business?"

Matt smiled again. "Thanks," he said, and turned to go down the steps. He did not hear the door close until he had reached his car.

Chapter Twenty-five

Benjamin Stafford flashed the light in Galen Morgan's eyes and gauged the pupillary response. The medical records on this patient all indicated that upon admission, pupil reaction was sluggish although equal bilaterally.

Now, he noted with satisfaction, constriction of the pupil was normal.

Abrahms had done his usual excellent work.

"Very good," he said aloud.

The nurse who had hovered at his side throughout the exam smiled as though personally responsible.

"Is Dr. Turner still in the hospital?" he asked.

"She's with the mother."

"All right." He stripped off the sterile gloves and tossed them into the wastebasket. "That's where I'll be, then, if you need me." He looked back at the boy. "I want to be called if he as much as blinks an eye . . . and I mean day or night."

"Yes doctor."

He had worked with Megan Turner only once before but he'd been impressed by both her professionalism and her keen diagnostic skill. She had, he thought, an almost intuitive sense about people that allowed her to pick up on seemingly minor complaints and track them to their source.

She was also very attractive.

When he opened the door into the ICU waiting room and saw Megan with his patient's mother, his first thought was that they could be sisters.

The same height, the same slender build, both with that rich dark hair that looked as if it must feel like silk. Only their eyes were different—Megan's eyes, he knew from memory, were hazel flecked with green, and even at a distance he could see that Mrs. Morgan's eyes were blue.

"Ben," Megan said and smiled.

The smile he remembered even more than the eyes and he recalled overhearing a nurse remark that Megan's patients loved her.

He couldn't say that he blamed them.

Chapter Twenty-six

"Knock knock."

Megan looked up to see Dave Levine standing in the doorway.

"Who's there?"

His face split into a grin. "Mr. Right?"

"I don't think I'd better go on with this," she said.

Dave came into the room and lowered his bulk into a chair across from her. "You could be missing the chance of a lifetime."

"Could be." She regarded him, smiling. "Why are you dressed like that?"

He looked down at his brightly-hued shirt; the colors seemed almost to pulse with life. "I have no sales resistance. Besides, it's my day off."

"Then why are you here?"

"Why are *you* here?" he countered.

"Point for Dr. Levine."

"Actually, I'm here because of Abrahms."

Her smile faded. "Is there news?"

"Yes and no. No, the police aren't saying anything, but . . ."

"But?"

"It's science fiction time . . ."

"What do you mean?"

"The good doctor's brain is missing."

For a second she only stared at him. "You've got to be kidding."

"Nope." He held his hand up. "Scout's honor."

"Dave," she said reasonably, "someone is putting you on."

"I don't think so."

"Where did you get your information?"

"A friend of mine who's a reporter . . ."

"For the Enquirer?"

"She's a very reliable source," he insisted. "Don't get jealous, by the way, we're only friends."

"I'll try to control myself."

"She was at the morgue when Abrahms was brought in."

"And?"

"She was still there when the autopsy was over. From what she told me, everyone was pretty excited about it . . . they forgot to keep their voices down."

Megan winced. She knew too well the tendency of those in the medical professions to talk about patients—or victims, she supposed, in the coroner's case—as if they were only a collection of body parts.

"Anyway, what she heard . . . what she told me . . . was that Abrahms' brain had been removed. His skull was empty when they cut it open."

"What do you mean? Wasn't it already . . ."

Dave shook his head. "I told you this was weird. There were two wounds on his head." He placed his fingers on his own head in demonstration. "And the brain had apparently been sucked out through them."

Megan felt sick.

David kept his fingers in place.

"Burr holes," he said.

Chapter Twenty-seven

Calvin Hall looked into the depths of a very tall beer, his sixth. He intended, for the first time in his life, to get stinking drunk. He'd arrived at the bar a few minutes after five and it was now only six-thirty, so, he calculated, if he had his seventh drink before seven he'd be well on the way to feeling good.

And he hadn't felt good since yesterday morning.

But that was what he'd come here to try to forget.

He hiccuped and then frowned. His stomach was a little queasy. Beer really didn't taste that good going down; having it come back up did not seem to be a pleasant prospect.

Maybe he should have eaten something first.

With that thought in mind, he began to paw through the bowl of mixed nuts on the table, looking for cashews.

He became aware that someone was standing in front of him, and he paused in his foraging to look up.

It was the waitress. "Another?"

"Yes," he said and thought, hell yes, but couldn't bring himself to say it.

He could drink their drink but he couldn't talk their language.

The waitress walked away.

He cast a surreptitious glance around the bar, wondering where those people came from.

Mostly male, the current population of the establishment seemed to have been culled from the proverbial dregs of the earth. No one looked to be very clean, and there was an abundance of tattoos in sight. Most of them wore black engineers' boots with, he suspected, steel toes.

Steel toes were very useful in settling points of disagreement.

Two women sat at opposite ends of the bar.

The one nearest him was a bottle blond, her hair frizzed out in an imitation of the punk look. Studying her, he thought it might be a grandchild who had inspired her to torture her hair. An old grandchild. She was squeezed into a black skirt and a midriff-baring top. It looked like she had wrinkled flesh-colored inner tube around her waist.

She won the bar beauty contest.

The other woman looked like she had done time. Her hair was cropped off, shorter than his own, and yet it somehow looked tangled and matted.

She wore a pink bow above her left ear.

The rest of her clothes were leather. Not the sleek, sensuous fashions favored by Hollywood—and Huntington Beach—but scuffed and grubby and about as sexy as the dead animal they came from.

But it was her face that made him shiver.

She looked like she could stick a knife in your gut, twist it until your intestines spilled out, and then sit down and have a Big Mac with her feet propped up on your steaming corpse.

A hard woman.

But at least she . . . and the rest of them . . . belonged. They fit here.

Calvin envied them.

He'd never really belonged anywhere.

He threw a handful of peanuts in his mouth and chewed. When his seventh beer came he drank quickly and then got up—just a little unsteadily—to leave. He was disappointed that the room didn't sway.

Wasn't he supposed to be dizzy?

Shouldn't he be laughing by now?

He wished that he'd paid closer attention when the people at work talked about getting drunk; he must have done something wrong.

At the door he turned for a last look at the place. Even if he hadn't managed to get drunk, he suspected that he might wish to get nostalgic about all this some day; his first bar.

"Have a hell of a good night," he said.

No one looked up.

The worst of it was, he hadn't forgotten what he wanted to forget.

He had checked every machine and every electronic device in ICU and none had malfunctioned.

The only conclusion that he could come to was that he was in some way responsible for the deaths.

Chapter Twenty-eight

John sat on the porch steps, eyes closed, and listened to the night sounds. Crickets, the distant whistle of a train, dogs barking. Except for the traffic, it could almost be a spring night on the farm.

Inside the house, Edana was finishing cleaning up after supper and Kerri had gone up to her room.

Ordinarily he would have helped in the kitchen, or maybe read a story to Kerri, but tonight there were too many things on his mind.

Galen for one. The boy had always strongly resembled Peter, and seeing him that way, so pale and still, had given him quite a turn. And all those contraptions around the bed made him nervous.

The doctors had told Edana that they were through the worst times and that Galen should start to come out of it soon. What would happen when he woke up, no one would say.

John tried not to think about paralysis and seizures, which had happened to the Decker boy back home.

And then there was Kerri.

Something was wrong there, he thought, and he

wasn't sure if he agreed with Edana's assessment that it was worry over her brother.

Worry might explain the child not eating, but why would she want to be alone all the time? It wasn't natural, to his way of thinking, that a little girl spend so much time with only herself for company.

Kerri had never been as outgoing as Galen, that was true, but neither had she ever been as removed or as self-involved as she was now.

And there was a faraway look in her eyes, sometimes, that chilled him to the bone.

Yet hadn't he read that the bond between twins was many times stronger than between other brothers and sisters? There'd been a case of twin boys, raised apart, who nonetheless lived almost identical lives. They married women who looked alike and shared the same first name, and eventually chose the same names for their children.

And then there'd been twin girls who had developed their own language that no one else could understand. The details were a little fuzzy in his mind, but it seemed to argue for a close connection between babies who had shared a womb.

Maybe Kerri was sharing Galen's suffering on some level they couldn't even comprehend.

John frowned. He never was much for that psychic stuff.

As for Edana, he wished to hell that she would sell the house and come back to Iowa with him. She was almost finished with her training, and she could be a nurse there as well as here. It would be better for all of them . . .

"Dad?"

He turned to see her standing in the doorway.

"You going back to the hospital tonight?" he asked.

"For a little while. Do you want to come along? If you do, I can call Jeff; he said he'd come over to sit with Kerri if I needed him."

"No . . . no need for that." It would take some doing to find a need for that, he thought. "I'm a little tired . . . I think I'll read for a bit and then turn in."

She smiled. "All right. I won't be gone long."

He watched the car's tail lights disappear down the street and went inside.

Kerri was already asleep when he checked on her. She had pushed all the covers off and lay with one leg off the side of the bed. Looking at her, he felt a twinge of guilt for thinking the things he'd been thinking.

She was just a child, after all.

He poured a glass of milk and stood drinking it, watching a television report about the death of that doctor. Edana had told him about it, but now they were saying that they were "positive" that the doctor was killed at the hospital.

An autopsy had been performed but the findings were being withheld pending further analysis.

"Crazy," he said, and switched off the set.

He would talk to Edana soon.

MONDAY

Chapter Twenty-nine

"What's the occasion?" Rita asked, surveying the plates and bowls heaped high with food.

Maggie looked up from arranging a tray of vegetables. "It's a wake for Dr. Abrahms."

"He wasn't Irish."

"I know, but I can't hold it against the dear man."

"You're not Irish either."

Maggie smiled. "Details." She gestured toward a stack of paper plates. "Help yourself."

"Thanks, but I'd better check Galen first."

"Okay, but I'd hurry if I were you . . . you know how fast food disappears around here."

Rita intended to wait until the rest of the nurses—and the respiratory therapists, who could smell food a mile away and always showed up, salivating, forks in hand—were done.

While the rest of them were clustered in the back room she bathed Galen. The cutdown above his left ankle seemed a little redder, a little more swollen than the night before, and she swore softly under her breath as she applied a clean dressing.

What did they do on days, anyway?

She unwound the cords from his arm, then watched as he burrowed his arm back among them.

"Okay," she said, and let him be.

The first thing she did when she went to eat was toss a paper napkin over the bowl of black olives.

She couldn't abide the things, not since she'd seen a television report on insects in food products. As it happened, she was opening a can of olives just as they showed a close-up of a cockroach and explained about acceptable levels of "insect parts" in food.

Just beyond her range of vision, she thought she saw something move in the open can . . .

Now she couldn't even look at a black olive without imagining a roach inside it, hidden from all but the most careful inspection.

And looking at an entire bowl of olives was just asking for trouble; her mind translated the image into a seething heap of insects . . .

No. The bowl was safely covered.

She scanned the rest of the food, evaluating the likelihood of contamination of each item.

Brownies she never trusted.

Potato salad made her think of potato bugs.

There was a rice dish that looked interesting, but weren't rice paddies fertilized with human excrement?

Lasagna? Who could trust cheese after what happened last summer?

Stuffed mushrooms?

No.

She settled, finally, for an orange.

When she went back to take the two a.m. vitals, Galen had spiked a temperature of 102. His face was flushed and damp, and his breathing was a little labored.

She ran to the phone.

Chapter Thirty

Ben Stafford carefully palpated along the Galen's inguinal region, and found what he was searching for. The inguinal lymph nodes were definitely swollen. Lymphadenitis, then, on top of the localized lymphangitis.

"All right," he said, "let's start him on antibiotics and moist hot packs, and elevate his leg."

"Do you want a C & S?"

He nodded. "It's probably streptococci, but we'd better be sure." Peeling off his sterile gloves, he regarded his patient. The elevated temperature had given the child a feverish appearance but there were no indications that he was in any pain.

Nor were there signs of the restlessness and agitation common to head trauma patients coming up from a comatose state.

Yet he thought he detected a difference in the boy's face. In an unconscious or even a sleeping patient, the facial muscles were relaxed, making the face look softer, even slack. And that had been the way the boy looked the first time he had seen him.

Now, however, there seemed to be tightness around

the eyes and mouth like that of someone feigning sleep.

He didn't think it at all likely that the child was doing so; he had probed the infected wound after he had removed the IV, checking for necrotic tissue, a procedure he knew would have been intolerable if the boy were conscious.

"Doctor?"

The nurse had returned with a collection kit for the C & S. She looked anxious, he thought, a little surprised. ICU nurses were known for their ability to stay calm in life-or-death situations; this was just a simple wound culture.

Then it occurred to him that it was more likely she was upset about the murder of Dr. Abrahms. Some of the rumors going around were unsettling, to say the least.

As he collected a sample of the exudate from the wound, he noticed that the nurse was holding Galen's hand.

Chapter Thirty-one

Paula couldn't sleep.

She'd never been a patient in a hospital before, unless being born in one counted, which she was sure it didn't, since being born was involuntary, and anyway, she'd been too young to remember anything.

There were a lot of sick people here.

Paula wasn't the least bit sick and she didn't particularly care for being around people who were. They tended to groan a lot and were always complaining about *something*. Then there was the smell . . .

It was depressing.

She thought they should have a special hospital just for people who weren't sick. Like a Club Medical or something. It would have to be closer to the beach, though.

She sighed and turned over in the bed for the hundredth time. If she didn't get to sleep soon she'd be a wreck when they came to get her for surgery.

She didn't want to look awful in the operating room; it was bad enough that the nurse had forced her to wash off all of her make-up, remove her jewelry and take off her false fingernails.

Well, she'd just have to sneak and put on a little mascara.

What the nurse didn't know . . .

She closed her eyes tightly and tried to will herself to sleep. They'd given her a pill that was supposed to help her relax enough to fall asleep, but she'd recognized it as a Valium and knew it wouldn't help, her tolerance was just too high.

"Come on," she said to herself, and flopped onto her back. The hospital gown was tangled up around her waist and she tugged at it.

Her hands found their way to her breasts.

In a few hours she would be a thirty-four C.

Bilateral augmentation mammoplasty. She had memorized the words that would change her life.

Boob job, her boyfriend called it.

She privately thought a boob job was any work or employment that *he* might qualify for. His lack of sensitivity really bothered her sometimes. Like the horror story he told her about a girl at school whose silicon implants kept sliding until they were in her armpits.

He seemed to forget that this was for his benefit, too.

Then again, maybe when the stitches were out and the swelling went down, she would go looking for someone with a little more class.

Cleavage was leverage, she knew.

Maybe someone who lived at the beach.

There were no two ways about it, she had to pee.

The nurse had told her not to get out of bed: "You've been medicated," the nurse had said, not knowing of course, that it would take more than five milligrams of Valium to affect her balance. "If you have to go to the bathroom, push the call light and I'll bring in a bedpan."

The thought of using a bedpan did not appeal to her.

Paula sat up in bed and looked out the open door into the corridor; no one was in sight.

Her roommate was sound asleep, snoring softly.

She swung her legs off the side of the bed and was startled, as her feet touched the floor, to hear the sudden loud clanging of an alarm.

Her first thought was that they were going too far; she was only just getting out of bed.

Then she realized that it was a fire alarm.

She'd made a mistake.

On hearing the alarm her immediate impulse was to run, get out of the building, and she'd taken off down the hall toward what she thought was safety.

Then the fire doors began to swing shut.

As they shut the light grew dimmer, and now she was blocked off and stranded in a dark, L-shaped section of the hall . . . with no other doors.

She huddled in a corner and listened to the incessant sound of the fire alarms.

Now she *really* had to pee.

Chapter Thirty-two

"Everything is fine now, dear." Rosemarie patted the patient's liver-spotted hand and tried to smile reassuringly. "I'm just going to give you your medication like your doctor ordered."

"Is the fire out?" the woman asked for the third time.

"There wasn't a fire, dear, it was only a false alarm."

"Is it out?"

Rosemarie could only smile in the face of such persistence. "Yes, dear, it's out."

The entire medical floor was in an uproar and the call board was lit up like a Christmas tree. Tremulous voices cried out in confusion, and several of the patients had gotten up and were even now wandering through the halls, their noses quivering as they sniffed for smoke.

And she was late with the six a.m. meds.

She checked the patient's wristband to make sure she was in the right room, and then turned to the medication cart.

Usually she prepared injections by the nurse's station, but with all of the traffic out there she thought it better to just roll the cart to the rooms and draw the medications up at the bedside.

She picked up the vial of Demerol and then looked for a disposable syringe, certain that she had put a box of them in the bottom drawer of the cart.

"Damn." They were nowhere to be found.

"Is it out?"

"I'll be right back, honey," she said, and started out the door.

At the nurse's station she asked the secretary if she had seen the box of syringes.

"You took them," the secretary said. "I saw you put them on the cart."

"They're not on the cart now."

"Did you check the drawers?"

She nodded. They stared at each other.

"I'll have to call central supply," the secretary said after a moment. "That was the last box we had."

"Well, tell them to hustle because we're already late as it is."

"The terms 'hustle' and 'central supply' are mutually exclusive, but I'll try."

Rosemarie hurried down the hall, the box of syringes held tightly under her arm.

The call lights were flashing.

Voices were calling.

Going into the first room she noted gratefully that the patient had fallen back asleep; something was going right for a change.

She ripped open the box and grabbed a handful of

the paper-wrapped syringes which she tossed on top of the cart. The box she shoved vengefully into the bottom drawer.

Working quickly, she attached a needle to the syringe and stuck the needle through the rubber seal of the medication vial. She pulled the plunger back and the drug was drawn into the barrel of the syringe.

After checking to make sure there were no air bubbles she turned to the patient and inserted the needle into the IV stopcock.

"Fire," the woman muttered in her sleep.

Rosemarie injected the medication into the intravenous line.

"One down, ten to go," she said and turned back to the medication cart. She jammed the soiled needle into the red disposal box and then tossed the barrel assembly into the trash.

The vial of medication was lying on its side and she picked it up . . . and paused.

There was a very odd gurgling sound behind her; she turned to see.

The patient's face was a dusky blue.

Rosemarie's eyes looked from the woman to the vial in her hand. It was not Demerol.

It was morphine.

A massive overdose of morphine.

Chapter Thirty-three

Edana watched as Kerri pulled on a pair of white anklets and then slipped her feet into her best black dress shoes.

"You don't have to go to school today if you don't want to," Edana said. "I can call your teacher."

"I want to go."

"I thought maybe you would like to come with me to the hospital, and then we could go out and have lunch somewhere, just the two of us."

"What about Grandpa?"

"He wants to spend a little more time with Galen." And I, Edana thought, need to spend some time with you.

Kerri frowned. "No . . . I think I'd better go to school. I don't want to get behind."

"You won't get behind in one day."

"There's a field trip today."

"There'll be other field trips."

"I want to go on this one."

"Kerri . . ."

Her daughter's expression was serious. "I want to go."

"All right," she said, a little exasperated, "you can go."

The phone rang just as she was cracking an egg into the skillet.

"Dad?"

John nodded and went to answer the phone. He was back in an instant, taking the spatula from her hand.

"It's for you . . . a Mrs. Brown."

Kerri and Galen's teacher.

"Mrs. Morgan, I heard about poor Galen's accident and I wanted to extend my sympathies . . ."

"Thank you."

"I know you must have a million things on your mind at a time like this, but I wondered if you'd be able to come by the school and pick up some assignments . . ."

"Assignments?"

"For Kerri," the woman continued. "She's a very smart little girl, I know, but missing school at this point in the term could set her back for a while."

"Mrs. Brown, Kerri will be at school today."

"What?"

"She wants to go to school."

"Oh my," she stammered, "I just assumed, with the family situation, that she'd be out for a week or so."

Edana said nothing, having thought the same thing.

"Well," the teacher continued, "then I guess . . . I'm sorry to bother you, Mrs. Morgan."

"It's no bother. Thank you for thinking of Kerri."

"And Galen, of course."

"Yes, Galen."

She wrote Kerri's name on the lunch bag and handed it to her. "Well, you're ready for school," she said.

Kerri nodded and started for the door.

"Kerri," John said, "aren't you forgetting something?"

Kerri dutifully kissed them both.

"Enjoy your field trip," Edana said.

"Field trip?" John looked from Edana to Kerri. "Where are you going?"

"The airport," Kerri said, and was gone.

Chapter Thirty-four

"When will they be ready for him in radiology?" Megan asked the nurse at the desk.

The nurse consulted a schedule, glanced at her watch, and then looked up. "His brain scan is scheduled for eight-thirty, so I imagine someone will be up to get him any minute now."

"Good . . . would you mind calling to make sure there'll be a technologist to keep an eye on the respirator?"

"Will do."

Megan thanked her and went back across the unit to where Edana Morgan was waiting with her son.

"It won't be long now," she said.

Edana touched Galen's face. "He's so warm."

"I don't think you need to worry; his temperature is coming down. I suspect it's a low-grade infection and the antibiotics should knock it right out."

"When he was younger," Edana said, brushing the hair back from the boy's face, "every time he ran a fever, he'd have the most awful nightmares . . . and wake up screaming. It always scared me to see him like that."

"I can imagine it would."

"But this . . . stillness . . . scares me more."

They both stood aside as Galen was transferred from the bed onto a gurney.

"Can I go with him?" Edana asked.

"I'm afraid not. Why don't you go have a cup of coffee? I'll ask the nurse to page you when his scan is finished."

"How long do you think it will be?"

"An hour at the most. Oh!" Megan dug in her pocket and pulled out a card. "I was asked to give this to you . . ." she glanced at the name on the card and handed it to Edana. ". . . by Officer Kennedy. He put his home number on the back."

". . . in case I can't reach him at the office."

"That's what he said," Megan agreed.

"I guess I'd better call him."

"Have him paged . . . he's here in the hospital."

Chapter Thirty-five

"Whoa, where are you going?"

The stretcher Paula was lying on came to an abrupt stop. She propped herself up on one elbow and looked sleepily at the nurse who had positioned herself between the stretcher and double doors marked "Room Two."

The orderly who was pushing the stretcher snapped his gum.

"In there," he said, "she's scheduled for a ten o'clock in O.R. two."

"Well, she's been bumped."

Paula frowned and lay back down. They had given her a shot of something and she was finding it hard to think, but she *thought* the nurse had said she'd been bumped. Like, on an airline?

"But they said you were ready for her."

"She's an elective and we've got an emergency surgery coming down from E.R. in about two minutes."

"So what do I do with her?"

"Put her over in the corner; room five might be clear in twenty minutes or so."

"Do I have to stick around too?"

"Do you like your job?"

Paula felt the stretcher move and she closed her eyes because looking at the ceiling move made her dizzy.

"So," the orderly said, "what's the emergency?"

"A woman with a dissecting aneurysm."

The orderly whistled.

Paula pouted, but she knew better than to complain to a nurse; when she was a kid, she'd had to have allergy shots, and every time she would even politely mention that the shots hurt, the nurses would practically ram the needle through her arm. No, it was wiser not to complain to any person who might have an opportunity to hurt you.

What she would do, she thought drowsily, was write a letter to the management and point out that *she* had scheduled her surgery weeks and weeks ago, and that it was very unfair of them to bump her because of some lady's aneurysm, whatever that was.

She heard the 'whoosh' of the electronic doors and then a booming male voice.

"Have they brought the mammoplasty down yet?"

That was her! She tried to wave her arm but it felt like warm mush. "Hello," she called.

"She's here, Dr. Edwards, but she's been bumped for a patient from E.R."

Edwards . . . that was the little man who'd come into her room last night and introduced himself as the 'gas passer.' She turned her head and opened her eyes as wide as she could. They were facing away from her.

"Why wasn't I notified?"

"It happened five minutes ago . . . there wasn't

136

time. Anyway, they're going to need you for the emergency patient."

"I don't suppose it's anything quick, like an appy."

"A dissecting aortic aneurysm."

"Shit."

Just then the doors whooshed open again and a crowd of people came in, all of whom seemed to be talking at the same time.

"Don't worry 'bout me," Paula said, feeling sorry for herself.

No one even heard her.

Paula drifted.

It was quiet now, and when she looked she saw that she was alone. Was it safe for them to leave her alone? In her condition?

She felt like crying, wanted to cry, but for some reason her tear ducts wouldn't cooperate. It was very annoying. She tried thinking of the sad things: the end of *Gone With the Wind*, her grandfather's funeral, those telephone commercials . . .

There was a commotion behind the doors of Room Two. Loud voices, and then a nurse came running out, really running, and took off down the hall.

Mildly curious, Paula turned onto her side.

The nurse came running back just then, pushing a big red thing that looked a lot like what Paula's father kept his tools in. When she pushed it through the doors Paula could make out what they were shouting:

"The blood's too dark . . ."

"She's not getting oxygen . . ."

"What the hell?"

Then the doors swung shut and there were only muffled voices again. Paula blinked and closed her eyes.

"What the hell happened in there?"

The voices were close to her now, much quieter. They must have thought she was alseep.

"I don't know."

Dr. Edwards' voice, but no longer booming.

"I had a chance to save that one," the first voice said. "Catch an aneurysm just as it blows, a long shot, and then you kill the patient."

"I didn't . . ." Edwards began.

"You asphyxiated her."

"There must have been something wrong with the oxygen lines . . . that's all I can say."

"The only thing wrong with those lines is that you forgot to pump oxygen through them."

"I know I turned that valve on."

"Tell that to the lady's husband and kids."

Silence.

A hand touching her arm.

"We're ready for you now, hon."

"Oh no," Paula said, surprised at how much effort it took to talk. "I've changed my mind. Take me back to my room."

"But . . ."

"Get me out of here or I'll scream." Even with a head full of cotton candy, she knew that she had narrowly escaped death.

A flat chest was something she could . . . would . . . live with.

Chapter Thirty-six

The hospital cafeteria was deserted and Edana sat alone at one of the corner tables, watching Matt Kennedy as he talked to a fellow policeman a few feet away.

Judging by their expressions, whatever they were talking about wasn't good.

Since Dr. Abrahms had been found murdered the entire hospital seemed like it was under siege. The nurses were edgy and she didn't blame them; the rumors floating around about the manner of the doctor's death were particularly gruesome.

According to the news she'd heard on the radio on her way to the hospital this morning, the police had no suspect and no leads in the case. And they refused to give an official cause of death.

Edana tried to recall Abrahms' face . . . and couldn't. He had been instrumental in saving Galen's life, and all she could remember of him was the sound of his voice when he'd talked to her after Galen came out of surgery.

No, that wasn't true. She remembered the spots of blood on his shoes.

She closed her eyes.

"Edana . . . Mrs. Morgan?"

She looked up at Matt Kennedy, a little startled. She had been somewhere else . . .

"I'm sorry that took so long."

He sat down opposite her and smiled, an engaging, almost little-boy smile that made him look younger and not much like a policeman at all.

"Was it about Dr. Abrahms?" It occurred to her, suddenly, that the police might want to talk to her about Abrahms, since she had spoken to him shortly before he was killed.

"Well, no, I'm not on that case . . ." he shrugged, "just police business. How's your son today?"

"The doctors are optimistic."

"I'm glad to hear it."

"Is this about Galen then?"

"Excuse me?"

"Did you want to talk to me about the accident?"

He hesitated. "No . . . not really."

Confused, she tried to read the expression in his eyes. "I'm sorry," she said after a minute. "I don't understand. I've been getting all kinds of messages that you wanted to see me. I have a collection of your business cards. I thought at first that it was the accident, then maybe it was about Galen's doctor, and now it's neither?"

Color rose in his face. "I'm sorry, Mrs. Morgan . . ." he began, clearly embarrassed.

Then she understood, and was flattered.

"Call me Edana," she said.

When the call came that Galen was back from his brain scan, Matt walked her up to ICU.

"Edana," he said as they neared the doors, "I know this isn't a good time for you . . ."

She shook her head. "It really isn't."

"All right . . . but I want you to call me if there's anything I can do. Anything. Or even if you just want to talk." He started to search in his pocket.

"I have your card," she said with a smile.

"And you'll call?"

"Yes."

Chapter Thirty-seven

The school bus smelled like vomit.

Kerri wrinkled her nose as she walked down the aisle and took a seat near the back. She placed her sack lunch and her sweater on the seat beside her to discourage anyone from sitting down, and then looked out the window.

"Everybody sit down," Mrs. Brown yelled a minute later. "Or this bus is not moving."

Around her the other kids scrambled for a place. No one asked to sit next to her.

Then there was a grinding noise and the engine roared, and the bus was underway. Kerri seldom rode the buses, since she and Galen walked to school, but she rather liked them and she opened her eyes to look out as they drove, enjoying the sensation of looking down at the traffic around them. She could actually see inside the cars, and it had amused her to watch people who didn't know they were being watched.

The weather had cleared and the sky was crystal blue after being washed by the rain. Kerri could feel the sun warming her and she leaned back in the seat and closed her eyes.

Galen always said she was like a cat that way; dozing in the sun, turned lazy by heat.

He said she had nine lives, too.

How many did he have, she wondered.

It was odd to be out of the classroom in the middle of the day; nothing really looked the same to her. She didn't *feel* the same either. She felt . . . free.

And it wasn't like on the week-ends or summer or Christmas, because then all of the others were free too. This was something special.

A breeze ruffled her hair and she turned into it, feeling it cool her face. The air smelled fresher, looked cleaner, and she could even see the mountains that often disappeared in a haze of smog.

Galen would like today, she thought.

They stopped at a small park to have lunch before going on to the airport.

"All right." Mrs. Brown stood in the front of the bus, blocking the door. "Before we get off I want you all to make sure you've got your lunches. We're going to walk—in pairs—over to those picnic tables." She pointed and all eyes turned in that direction. "No running. We have twenty minutes to eat and then . . ." she gave them her no-nonsense look, ". . . we're getting back on the bus. That means if you run off to play, you might get left behind. Is that clear?"

No one answered although a few, Kerri noted, nodded their heads.

"Is that clear?"

A chorus of "Yes, Mrs. Brown," rippled through the packed aisle.

"All right." She stepped aside.

Forty-three of her classmates ran and jumped, heading pell-mell toward the swings and monkey bars.

Mrs. Brown looked at her. "Thank God, Kerri, at least you listened."

Kerri always listened.

The driver parked the bus on a side street across from the airport and again Mrs. Brown blocked the door.

"We are going to have to cross a very busy street to get to the airport and I want you all to get off the bus and then line up—in pairs—on the sidewalk before we walk down to the corner. I would hate," she said, "to have to call your mothers and tell them that you ran across MacArthur Boulevard and were hit by a car . . ." She stopped abruptly and frowned.

Kerri looked out a window.

"Just stay in line and keep up," Mrs. Brown finished lamely.

The airport was not what she'd imagined.

There were people everywhere and Kerri noticed that she and her classmates, in straggly rows of two, were receiving a lot of irritated looks.

Mrs. Brown and the room mothers kept moving them along from one place to another. At each point of interest they clustered around and listened as the

144

teacher explained what they were looking at.

They looked at a ticket counter, gates that looked nothing like a real gate, the baggage claim area, a small giftshop, the stairway leading up to the airport restaurant (Mrs. Brown wouldn't let them go up), and, since it was a long time until they would get back to school, the bathrooms.

One of the boys tried to jump on the conveyor belt that passed through the X ray machine.

Mrs. Brown was losing her voice.

Kerri found it boring.

Outside they lined up along a wire fence to watch the planes take off. They had to wait through three small planes before they saw a big one.

It was too noisy when the big one took off to hear what the teacher was saying, and Kerri yawned, her eyes following the plane as it angled up into the sky. It looked to her like it might fall back to earth but it didn't.

She didn't like the little planes.

Not at all. They made an annoying sound and she remembered the times at home when they flew overhead, their noisy engines whining like angry insects.

She held onto the fence and closed her eyes, imagining the planes falling out of the sky.

"Oh God!"

They were walking back toward the bus and all turned to look at what Mrs. Brown saw.

A small plane coming down practically beneath an

airliner and then rising up until it seemed it would crash into the belly of the bigger plane.

Around her some of the children screamed.

"Oh!"

Kerri looked at Mrs. Brown who now had her hands over her mouth.

The big plane started to pull up but its landing gear hit the small plane's left wing . . .

The small plane seemed to spin in the air and then it disappeared from their view. The airliner continued to pull up, straining, moving ever so slowly up and away.

Black smoke was visible now and the fire sirens could be heard over the sound of the traffic.

With all of the excitement, it was three o'clock before they got back to the schoolyard.

It had been, Kerri thought, a better than usual day.

She walked home alone.

Chapter Thirty-eight

John left the hospital early so that he would be at the house when Kerri got home from school, but when she arrived, contrary to his expectations, she went straight up to her room and closed the door.

So much, he thought, for heart-to-heart talks.

He'd told Edana that he would make supper for them tonight so he went into the kitchen and pulled the bag of game hens out of the refrigerator.

Four of them, since Garrett had been invited.

He'd kept his peace when Edana mentioned that her friend was coming, and he figured he could keep a hush on through supper as well, but the time was coming when he'd have to speak his mind.

It wasn't that he didn't want her to see other men; Peter wouldn't have wanted her to spend her life alone and neither did he. Chauvinist or not, he believed that a woman needed a man, particularly when there were kids to be raised.

But it had to be the *right* man and his instincts told him that Garrett wasn't it.

True, he'd only just met the man, but he'd learned in his lifetime that first impressions often told the true story. Folks could yammer all day long about not judging a book by its cover but in his experience what you saw was what you got.

And he didn't like what he saw.

Finding a man who measured up to Peter would take some doing, but Edana deserved nothing less.

He would see to it.

They arrived together a little after five, Garrett pulling up behind Edana in his little foreign car.

Watching them out the kitchen window, he was gratified to see that his daughter-in-law merely held her hand out to Garrett instead of hugging him. Garrett, for his part, offered her a single red rose.

That was California for you; one rose.

He turned from the window and went into the hall, remembering just in time to take off the apron.

All through dinner he had to look at that rose, sitting in a bud vase in the center of the table.

"What's wrong, Dad?" Edana asked. "You're awful quiet."

"Just tired, I suppose."

"Jet lag," Garrett suggested.

He glared at their dinner guest. "Tired," he repeated.

Edana looked concerned. "Why don't you lie down for a little while?"

He waved it off. "I'll be fine."

"Mr. Morgan, if you're tired I can drive Edana back to the hospital this evening."

That he didn't need. "Wouldn't think of it."

"I'll be glad to do it."

Persistent little bastard, he thought. "Edana," he said, as if Garrett hadn't spoken, "you never told me what the policeman wanted."

"Policeman?"

John glared at Garrett.

"Oh," Edana said, "it was nothing at all. He just wondered how Galen was doing."

"Is this the same policeman who left his card yesterday?"

There was something in the tone of Garrett's voice that John could not decipher. He looked from one to the other.

"Hmm?"

Garrett leaned back in his chair, a hint of a smile on his face. "The same policeman . . . what was his name? Kennedy?"

Edana lowered her eyes. "Matt Kennedy, yes."

"And he wanted to ask how Galen was?"

"Well . . ."

"He came to the house on Sunday to leave a card, with his home phone number on it . . . so he could ask you how Galen was? He couldn't just call the hospital?"

John felt like he was at a tennis match, looking back and forth between them.

"Well, he . . ."

"And then today he followed you to the hospital?"

"He didn't *follow* me . . . he was there and we happened to see each other."

John thought it was time to put in his two cents worth. "He left his card for you with the doctor, didn't he?"

"Ho!" Garrett laughed.

The laugh he didn't understand.

"Sounds like the officer is in hot pursuit," Garrett teased.

"Jeff!" Edana was blushing.

John caught the glance between them and added it to the list of things he didn't understand. Why would a man laugh if he suspected, as Garrett clearly did, that another man was interested in the woman he was seeing?

It's California, he thought.

Chapter Thirty-nine

"Coming to bed soon?"

Willie looked up from the television.

Ray stood in the doorway and yawned, rubbing his bare stomach with one hand.

He looked very good in just his pajama bottoms.

"Soon," she said.

Instead of going back in the bedroom, he joined her on the couch. "So what's new in the world?"

"More of the same."

"Death and debauchery."

"Among other things." She looked back at the screen; a body was being loaded into the back of a coroner's van. The sound was off—it was the only way she could watch the news—but the caption indicated the film, and maybe the body, had been shot in Pasadena.

"It's your night off," Ray reminded her.

"I just can't sleep now."

"Why don't you tell me what's bothering you?"

She looked at him, surprised. They had only been living together for two months now and had only known each other for a few weeks before that, and his sensitivity to her moods was uncanny.

Instead of answering, she snuggled into his arms and kissed his bare chest.

Maybe it would work out between them, and maybe it wouldn't, but she would never regret giving it a chance. None of the complications that she'd worried about—including his being white—had mattered so far, and she almost believed that, for once, love was enough.

"Is it work?"

It was tempting to say that it was. With all that had happened in the last few days—the crash of the air ambulance, Abrahms' death, the deaths in ICU, the drug overdose on medical floor, malfunctioning fire alarms—it would be easy to ascribe all of her depression to her job.

But they had promised each other to be honest, and she knew that even if he didn't know that she was lying to him, *she* would know.

Yet how could she explain about Galen Morgan? How?

She felt his hands caress her shoulders and she sighed, wondering how and where to start. At the beginning, she decided, the true beginning . . . when she was a child.

"It's a long story," she said finally, and moved back so that she could see his face.

"We've got all night."

"I grew up in a little town in the Santa Cruz mountains, Ben Lomand, not too many people have heard of it. It wasn't much of a town, mostly just houses scattered here and there, a gas station, a store . . . a quiet place. Mama and I were the only black people living there that I knew of, but like I said, it was kind of spread out, so maybe I'm wrong."

Ray smiled and kissed the palm of her hand. "You're never wrong."

"Anyway, we lived in a little house that clung to the side of a hill; there was a wood stairway in back of the house that went down to the creek bed below us. I used to play all day, running up and down those stairs." She paused and looked at him. "You're probably wondering what all this has to do with anything . . ."

"Everything has to do with everything else. Go on."

In a minute she did. "I guess what I'm trying to say is that I was alone a lot. The nearest neighbor was about a mile away . . . most of the neighbors were just summer people anyway. Mama was working, and I had to keep myself entertained."

"Poor baby."

"I managed," she said dryly. "It's a wonder I didn't bring the house down around my ears. Anyway, I was alone a lot of the time. I guess it made an impression on me, because when I was five or so, I asked Mama to have another baby so I'd have someone to play with."

"What about the kids at school?"

"I was born in December, so I didn't start school until I was almost six."

"What did your mother say?"

"Well, Mama had never married my father, and she told me she couldn't have a baby by herself. *That* I didn't understand at all . . . she was always telling me how she was by herself when I was born."

153

Roy smiled. "Did you call her on it?"

"I did, but she would only say she'd tell me later, and to forget about another baby. So I asked for a puppy instead."

Now he laughed. "Did you get it?"

"I got it, but it only confused me more . . . Mama took me to a kennel to pick out the puppy, and I asked the man where was the daddy dog. He said he didn't have the daddy and explained that he'd taken the mother dog to a breeder . . . I don't remember for sure, but I imagine that I gave my mother any number of significant looks while he was telling us about dog breeding."

"Willie," Ray said, "I would've loved to have seen your mama's face."

"Anyway, I got my puppy and later that year I started school and there were other kids to play with . . . and it wasn't enough. It took a few years before I could really put words to my feelings, but I felt like I was missing a part of myself. And that was what I was lonely for."

Ray leaned across and kissed her gently.

"When I was twelve, Mama told me that I was a twin."

"Oh Willie."

"I'd had a sister who'd died at birth." Even after living with it for twenty years, it hurt to say it.

Ray was silent, waiting for her to continue.

"Her name was Wilona and Mama said we were identical right down to our toes. She hadn't wanted to tell me about Wilona until I was old enough to understand . . ." She sighed. "I still don't understand."

He gathered her up in his arms and held her, kissing the top of her head.

They sat that way for a time and Willie waited, dry-eyed, for the ache to go away. She'd never told anyone before . . .

"So how is it now?" he said quietly, not letting her go.

"I live with it. And sometimes weeks go by and I never think of her at all, and then when I do I feel guilty for forgetting."

"Is that what's been bothering you, then?"

"In a way. There's a patient at the hospital . . . his name is Galen Morgan . . . and he's a twin."

"What's he in for?"

"He was hit by a car on Friday, he's in ICU."

"Oh no."

"The thing is . . . I was working at the hospital when he and his sister were born. They were premature and there was a time when the doctors thought they might not make it. I used to go up and look at them after I got off work. There was something about them . . . I was almost desperate for them to live."

"I think that's understandable."

"I'm sure the psychiatrists could have a field day explaining my feelings about them, how I identify with them. All I know is that I care."

"Is he . . . is Galen . . ." his voice faltered and she pulled back, looking at his face and knowing the question that he was finding so hard to ask.

"He's holding his own," she said, the words an echo of the time so many years ago. "The doctors say he'll probably make it."

"That's good, then."

She nodded slowly. "It is, I know."

"So what's wrong?"

I'm frightened, she thought, but don't know why. What explanation was there for the mixed feelings of love and fear that battled within her when she looked at Galen Morgan's face? He was just a child.

Instead of answering she brought her hand up, stroking his face. She searched his eyes and saw his questions give way to desire.

Without a word, he got up from the couch and held out his hand to her.

Later, long after he had fallen asleep, she lay awake wondering about the boy's sister.

Kerri.

Chapter Forty

The Death Committee met Tuesdays at ten a.m.

Calvin looked at the clock and imagined he could hear it ticking away the seconds of his life. It was nearly midnight.

In a little over ten hours, the finger of blame would be pointing at him. The autopsy reports on the two patients who died would be presented to the Committee which would then reach the only conclusion possible: he had killed them.

Accidentally killed them, but that didn't make them any less dead.

He would be summoned to the meeting room . . .

It didn't seem likely that he would be arrested, at least not yet, but he knew he would be suspended or maybe fired. At some point, he feared, he would be charged with manslaughter and then it was possible, or rather probable, that he would be taken to jail.

At best he would be found guilty of criminal negligence.

The families would sue either way.

It was how Americans recouped their losses.

He had not gone in to work this morning, had not even gotten dressed. Shades drawn, he sat in the dark, trying to figure a way out.

If there was a way clear he hadn't found it.

Time was running out.

All of his life he had been good at finding solutions, blessed with a faultlessly logical mind. He had always felt equal to any challenge.

Decisive, that's what he was.

But now it was obvious that he was up against something beyond his control. His fate was no longer in his hands. He would have to stand by while others—first the Committee, then the police, and finally a judge—passed judgment on him.

The feeling of impotence was not one he enjoyed.

How had all this happened to him?

When had he lost control?

Calvin paced around the small apartment, stopping at each window to peak out, looking for, he knew, salvation.

He wished there was someone he could talk to. Maybe talking about his fears would defuse them.

Who did he know who might be willing to listen?

At this hour of night? No one.

"Wait," he said out loud, and looked wildly around him for the phone.

A crisis hotline.

He found the phone where he had hidden it under the sofa cushions—it had rung all morning and he knew it was the hospital wondering where he was—and grabbed the phone book.

158

Would it be under 'crisis' or 'hotline'?

Just then he remembered the sheet of numbers in the back of his hospital orientation manual.

"I hope you'll never need them," the director of personnel had said, "but remember that you represent the hospital to the community, and you should always be prepared to help out in any situation."

The manual he located under the bed; it was very effective as a sleep aid.

There were dozens and dozens of numbers.

Rape crisis, family crisis, drug crisis, alcohol crisis . . .

None of them were really what he needed.

Suicide intervention.

The word struck him like a rush of cold water in the face.

Suicide.

His eyes began to sting and he rubbed at them and took his hand away and saw that there were tears.

No. It was insane. Even if he went to jail, it wouldn't be for long. And when he got out, he could start again. He would have a second chance.

They didn't get a second chance.

The telephone beeped in his ear as he pushed the buttons to place his call.

"Crisis intervention, can you hold?"

Before he could answer, he heard the click and the nothing sound of dead air.

No. That was a joke. Comedians joked about calling suicide prevention and being put on hold.

It was a joke.

He hung up the phone.

He didn't have a gun, didn't believe in sleeping pills, had a safety razor. The stove was electric. He knew he couldn't drive his car off a cliff.

He did have a rope.

The note was only seven words.

TUESDAY

Chapter Forty-one

Kirsten wrapped the phone cord around her finger and stared up at the ceiling, listening as the voice babbled in her ear. Did the woman never breathe? More pertinent, didn't she ever sleep? It was almost one o'clock in the morning!

"Yes, Rita," she interrupted, "I'll be sure and take a look, but like I said, it's pretty busy here and I don't really have time to talk."

That wasn't true; two patients had been transferred out of the unit on the p.m. shift and the nurse-patient ratio was nearing the one-to-one ideal.

"Yes, I'll call you if anything changes." Kirsten hung up the phone and blew out an audible sigh of relief.

The other nurses standing around the desk looked at her curiously.

"Rita," was her one word explanation.

"Again? How many times has she called tonight?"

"This was number four. Four calls in two hours time."

"What did she want?"

"Where should I start? She wants me to give him a

bath . . ."

"Him?"

Kirsten gestured absently. "Morgan. Then I'm supposed to change the sheets, change his gown, scrub the bed. You name it. Why she's calling on her night off . . ."

"Maybe she's bucking for nurse of the year," someone suggested.

"Pain in the ass of the year, *that* she'll win." Kirsten pulled a chart across the desk toward her and flipped through to the progress report.

"It's funny . . ."

Kirsten looked up to see who was talking; it was Maggie, one of the older ICU nurses. "Funny?"

"I've worked with Rita for about two years now, and I've never known her to get so involved with a patient." Maggie turned to look at the little boy.

"Does she have kids of her own?"

"No," Maggie said thoughtfully, "and I'd wager she never wanted any."

"Why do you say that?" Kirsten was curious; her own quick assessment had been that Rita was one of those Super Moms, women who were totally fixated on children, theirs or anyone else's.

"She just never seemed interested in kids. When people would start showing pictures, you could see the lack of enthusiasm on her face. In fact, I remember her saying that kids all looked alike to her . . ."

Kirsten, who had often thought the same thing, nodded.

"Maybe," one of the other nurses suggested, "he resembles her brother or something. I took care of a lady once who looked just like one of my aunts and it

164

was hard to keep objective."

"I guess anything is possible," Maggie agreed.

Kirsten got up from the chair and tucked the chart under her arm. "Well, I guess I'd better take care of little Prince Charming. No point in postponing the inevitable."

Kirsten drew the curtains around the bed.

"So, Galen," she said, coming up to the side rail and lowering it. "Work your magic on me."

He lay perfectly still.

She eyed him critically. Cute, she supposed, for a kid. The bruises on his face were beginning to lighten and change color, a process which had always fascinated her, since she was herself a kid, and which had, to a minor degree, influenced her decision to become a nurse.

She could remember wondering about whether blood was really red all of the time or whether, as her cousin insisted, it was blue until exposed to the air.

"Arteries and veins are clear," Marty said, "so they must get the blue color from somewhere."

The thought of blue blood circulating within her made her feel kind of alien, like Mr. Spock.

She'd never found out for sure, since she was too embarrassed to ask the teacher when she was in nursing school. Still, you'd think the truth would come out, sooner or later.

Taking hold of the boy's wrist, she turned it and held her index and middle fingers over the vein, finding the pulse. She looked at her watch.

His pulse was strong and steady.

Kirsten frowned and loosened her hold on his wrist, losing count. She had a sudden weird feeling she was being watched. A quick glance verified that the curtains were tightly drawn.

Then she looked at the boy's face.

He was watching her with violet-blue eyes.

Chapter Forty-two

Rita knew something was happening at the hospital that Kirsten hadn't told her about. She could feel it in the marrow of her bones. Her anxiety had intensified with each passing moment until now she felt near hysteria.

Galen needed her.

She would have to go to him.

Hurrying into her bedroom, she grabbed a pair of jeans and a blouse and began to dress, her fingers clumsily struggling to fasten buttons and pull up the zipper. She slipped her feet into a pair of sandals, unmindful of the chilly February night, and, forcing the straps over her heels, she half-ran toward the front door.

Just in time—just as the door was closing—she realized that she had left her purse and keys inside. She had come that close to locking herself both out of the apartment and out of her car.

"Calm down," she told herself.

Her purse was where she always left it, hanging from a peg in the hall closet. Even in her present state she felt a momentary satisfaction at how her personal neatness made her life so predictable.

The car was completely fogged in and she let the motor run while she used the wiper on all of the windows.

She was the only one in the carport and the sound of her breathing was loud to her ears. Last summer, only a few feet away from where she now stood, a woman had been attacked and raped.

Since that incident she had avoided coming out here late at night; her twelve hour shift from 7 p.m. to 7 a.m. enabled her to leave for work while people were still coming home. But now her fear for Galen was far greater than her fears for her own safety, and she would not even allow herself a cautionary look around at the shadows.

When the windows were clear she tossed the wiper into the back seat and jumped in the car, jamming the gear shift into drive and taking off with a squeal of the tires.

It usually took her fifteen minutes to drive to work. Tonight she was there in nine.

The security guard stationed near the emergency room entrance looked at her, recognized her and went back to his crossword puzzle.

She hurried through E.R. and turned down the hall toward the back elevators. Both elevators were, according to the indicators, down in the basement, and she realized the central service was probably loading the supply carts for the floors.

There was no time to wait for them.

When she pulled open the door into the fire stairwell, she thought briefly of Dr. Abrahms, knowing from the talk that he'd been killed a floor below. The

168

danger, however, seemed minimal compared to her urgency to reach the boy.

Her footsteps were the only sound she heard.

"My God!"

Rita had burst through the door and almost collided with a nurse coming out of the coronary care unit. The nurse looked at her peculiarly.

"Sorry," she said, breathless.

"Visiting hours," the nurse started to say and then squinted at her. "You work here, don't you?"

The hall was poorly lit and Rita was vaguely surprised that the nurse recognized her, especially since she was not wearing a uniform.

"Excuse me," she said, and began to run down the hall toward ICU.

"What . . . ?"

As she neared the unit she slowed down to a walk, trying to catch her breath. She had a stitch in her side and she rubbed at it while trying to think of what she would say to the other nurses.

But when she pushed the door open it was clear that, for now at least, no one would ask her any questions.

All of them were standing around Galen's bed, watching as Dr. Turner removed the respirator connector from the tracheotomy tube.

Galen was breathing on his own.

Chapter Forty-three

Megan stood back watching the steady rise and fall of the boy's chest.

"Looks good," she said.

"Do you want me to leave this?" One of the therapists patted the respirator.

"For now." Her eyes moved to Galen's face; he appeared to be asleep.

"He *did* look at me," a young nurse said.

Megan did not comment. Coma patients often opened their eyes, but there was a world of difference between that purely physical action and really looking at someone with awareness.

She took the penlight out of her pocket and went to the head of the bed. Gently she raised his eyelids and flashed the beam into his eyes. The pupils constricted but did not follow the light when she moved it.

All of the physical findings indicated that he was still in a coma; the only thing that had changed, as far as she could determine, was that now he was breathing on his own.

They had planned to start weaning him from the respirator in the next day or so, but he had beat them to it.

A good sign, she thought.

"Do you want me to call his mother?" the nurse asked.

Megan shook her head. "To a mother with a child in the hospital, a phone call in the middle of the night could only mean something terrible's happened. It can wait till morning."

When she went out into the hall she caught a glimpse of someone ducking around a corner.

In this light it was hard to tell, but she thought that the person looked very much like Rita.

Chapter Forty-four

Edana ran upstairs, the newspaper in hand, and hurried down the hall to Kerri's bedroom. Her heart was pounding as she tapped lightly and then opened the door to her daughter's room.

Kerri, standing in front of the vanity mirror, looked at her in surprise.

"Kerri," she said, her mouth dry, "why didn't you tell me about the crash at the airport yesterday?"

"What?"

Edana felt a flash of anger. "Don't pretend that you don't know what I'm talking about . . . there's a comment from your teacher right here," she pointed at the article, "and it says that 'several of the second-grade students witnessed the crash.' "

Kerri's expression was unreadable. "I was going to tell you," she said vaguely.

For some reason her daughter's off-hand attitude irritated her. "A man was killed," she said, "and it could have been a lot worse . . . all of those people on the other plane."

Kerri averted her eyes, and gazed instead into the mirror.

Edana felt she had to persist. "And if the other plane had crashed too, there's no telling who might have been injured or killed on the ground."

Kerri gave no indication that she had even heard what Edana was saying.

The tightness increased in Edana's chest. "Kerri . . . you could have been hurt." She couldn't bring herself to say the other. "Don't you think I have a right to know when you've been that close to . . . to . . ."

"Death?"

The word out of her daughter's mouth sounded obscene.

Kerri faced her with just a hint of a smile. "I wouldn't have died," she said.

Edana ached inside. "I've lost your father, and I almost lost you and Galen when you were born, and now . . . the doctors say that your brother's doing better, but it was so close, Kerri. He could have died."

"Well I won't."

Hating it, she knew nonetheless that she had to say it. "No one ever knows when they might die. Galen didn't . . ." She was stopped cold by the look on her daughter's face.

For a long silent moment, their eyes held.

Edana was the first to look away.

She stood at the kitchen window and watched her daughter walk down the street alone.

There were other children on the block, but neither Kerri nor Galen had ever made friends with any of them. It was natural, Edana had always thought, that they should prefer each other's company, but now she wondered.

She knew from talking to their teachers that it was the same at school.

Kerri disappeared around the corner and Edana turned away to see John watching *her*.

"Anything wrong?" he asked.

"I wish I knew."

Driving to the hospital, she tried to shake the feeling that something was dreadfully wrong.

It was mother's anxiety, she told herself. She was over-reacting. There was nothing to be gained by worrying over 'could have beens.' The incident was over.

It was foolish of her to scold Kerri for not telling her about the crash; Kerri hadn't been injured, after all.

And Kerri's indifference regarding the death of the pilot of the small plane . . . didn't the experts say that children had become desensitized by all of the death and violence they witnessed on television and in movies?

Death didn't seem real to them, the experts said.

As much as she would have liked to accept such an explanation for her daughter's behavior, Edana wondered.

The look in Kerri's eyes . . .

Chapter Forty-five

Sunlight streaming through the venetian blinds.

Sounds of traffic filtering in from the street.

Doors slamming and footsteps in the hall, bits of conversation as people passed outside.

The phone ringing.

Calvin Hall opened his eyes to confront the mounting evidence.

He was alive.

"Damn it," he said, sitting up quickly and looking around the room. One of the kitchen chairs was positioned beneath an overhead light fixture from which hung the rope. The noose was definitely empty.

Staring at the noose and rubbing his neck, he struggled to remember. What had happened last night? His neck wasn't sore, so he thought it unlikely that he had tried to hang himself and failed.

Looking at the light fixture, he changed that 'unlikely' to 'definitely had not'; it clearly wouldn't have held his weight, and if he *had* tried, the whole lot of it—including himself—would be in a heap on the floor.

Not dead, but certainly wounded.

"Damn," he repeated and got to his feet slowly, feeling his muscles protest after having slept on the loveseat. "A little stiff this morning."

That struck him as enormously funny.

"A little stiff," he snorted, and circled the chair that was to have been the platform of his doom. He yanked the rope down which set the bargain basement chandelier to swaying.

The noose, at least, looked like it meant business.

What now, he wondered. Try again?

The prospect did not appeal to him. In fact the whole idea, in the clear light of morning, seemed asinine. What good would it do to kill himself? Would it bring those people back from the dead? No, it would not. Ergo, it was a stupid idea.

He carted the chair back into the kitchen and threw the noose in the linen closet and contemplated what to do.

The only logical thing to do, he decided, was to go to the hospital, sneak into the room where the meeting was scheduled, and listen to the committee as they determined his fate. It was better than cowering here in the apartment, waiting for a knock at the door.

There was no one in the meeting room when he arrived at a quarter to ten.

Where to hide?

He couldn't hide under the table . . . it was plexiglass.

The podium was a modern-looking, inverse pyramid-shaped contraption which might shield him from view if he could stand on his head indefinitely.

It was still technically winter and the doctors might be wearing coats, so the closet was out.

Curtains, he thought, and turned to look at them.

They were perfect. A rich burgundy color, they were heavy and lined to keep out the daylight on those occasions the doctors had a film to watch.

What kind of films, he wondered, did a Death Committee watch?

He stepped behind the curtains and pressed himself against the wall.

A few minutes later he heard the door open and the committee members began to file in.

It was all over in a matter of minutes.

Calvin was giddy with relief.

Neither he nor the computer had even been mentioned in connection with the ICU deaths.

One had died of a pulmonary embolism, the other of a massive myocardial infarction, according to the coroner, and the committee was satisfied with both determinations.

In fact they spent most of the time talking about the cases they would review at the next meeting; a death from an anesthesia error and a drug overdose.

He peeked around the curtain to make sure that all of them were gone and then came out, his legs a little rubbery now that the pressure was off.

One of these days, he thought, he would look back at this and laugh.

One of these days, the fact that he had almost

killed himself—for nothing—would seem amusing to him.

Right now, he couldn't imagine when that day would be.

He decided to give getting drunk a second chance.

Chapter Forty-six

"You can go right in, Dr. Turner," the secretary said, "he's expecting you."

"Thank you."

Terence Nolan looked up when she entered the office. "Megan, I'm glad you could spare me a few minutes of your time." He stood and indicated a chair opposite his desk.

"I thought it was a command performance."

"I wouldn't say 'command,' but it *is* urgent. I've already talked to several other doctors and I have a list of appointments with many more."

Curious, Megan sat down.

"These," the hospital administrator said, holding up a sheaf of papers, "are incident reports filed in the past three days." He paused. "Three days. In specific, this past Saturday, Sunday and Monday."

Megan waited, knowing there was more to come.

Nolan regarded her, as if searching for the answer to a yet unspecified question.

"There have been as many reports filed in the past three days as were filed in the entire *month* before then."

Megan frowned. "I had no idea . . ."

"I've got reports here on incidents . . ." he consulted the reports and began to read from them, "a faulty fire alarm system, elevators getting stuck between floors, an anesthesia death in surgery, a drug overdose, a computer malfunction in ICU, one of the centrifuges in lab is ejecting test tubes . . . totally against the laws of physics, I might add . . . and it goes on." He paused. "Even the incidents which were relatively minor had the potential to be much worse; when the fire alarms went off, some of the patients were scared half to death . . . and I don't blame them a bit."

"No, neither do I."

"And the worst of it isn't covered in these reports. Dr. Abrahms' death . . . murder . . . is not considered an 'incident.' Neither is the crash of the air ambulance the other night, since it didn't happen on hospital grounds. But the fact of the matter is, those deaths reflect on the hospital as well. And if you count up the lives lost in the past three days," he ticked them off on his fingers, "Abrahms, five aboard the helicopter, the one in surgery, the OD . . . that's eight people . . . it adds up to trouble for the hospital."

"More than that," Megan protested. "I hope that you're not regarding this as a public relations problem . . ."

"No, not at all. But trouble, in my experience, perpetuates itself. I think, and our staff psychiatrist thinks, that it is possible that concern about the murder and the other more . . . spectacular incidents may be contributing to the perpetuation of these incidents . . . by demoralizing certain members of the

180

staff who have then gone on to make what can only be called . . . inexcusable mistakes."

"Inexcusable by whose standards?" Megan asked.

"By the hospital's standards."

"I think it's easy to make judgments when you're standing outside looking in. It's a little harder to make life or death decisions on demand. There is such a thing as human error."

Nolan smiled. "I agree with you, in theory at least. But the fact remains that nurses and doctors are trained to make those decisions. When they deviate from written policy and standard procedures, and that deviation results in injury or, in some instances, death, to a patient, their actions are inexcusable. By anyone's standards."

"I'm at a disadvantage," Megan said. "I haven't read the reports, and I don't know what decisions were made, but I find it unacceptable for you—who are not a doctor—to term the decisions 'inexcusable' out of hand."

Nolan kept his face expressionless.

"We have," Megan continued, "an established method to evaluate nurse and physician performance, and I think it would be best for all concerned if determinations as to culpability, if any, were left to those qualified to judge."

Nolan held up his hands in surrender. "You're right, of course, although you will have to admit that the record of physicians policing themselves has been less than perfect."

His point, Megan knew, was valid; last summer the hospital had been in a turmoil after one of the local papers ran a series of articles on doctors protecting other doctors from disclosure of incompetence, even though the alleged acts of incompetence had resulted in patient deaths.

Cover-up was the term the newspaper had used, and it fit.

"Regardless," Nolan said, "there have been far too many unusual incidents in the past few days, and my intention in asking you here this morning, is to alleviate, and not aggravate, what is clearly a dangerous situation." He fanned the stack of papers. "I'm not hunting heads; I'm looking for help." He looked directly at Megan. "I need your help."

"What can I do?"

Back in the doctor's lounge Megan stared at the copies of the incident reports that Nolan had given her, troubled.

It all centered on Dr. Abrahms.

No matter what the administrator said about the murder not being part of the pattern, it was, she felt certain, at the core of it all.

The other incidents all could be blamed on mechanical failure or human error.

Abrahms' death, however, required intent.

Malicious intent.

What if, she wondered suddenly, that same intent was behind all of the incidents, and the killer was just getting better at hiding his acts?

In that case the incidents would continue until the person responsible was caught.

Chapter Forty-seven

Working as a registry nurse was the smartest decision Debbie had ever made.

When she'd gotten her R.N. she had done what nurses traditionally did; went to work for a hospital. There she quickly discovered that she hated the politics that went with being a staff nurse, hated being scheduled for hours and days that suited the hospital's needs and ignored her own, and most of all hated working with the same people, day in, day out.

The registry was the antidote to all that ailed her.

It was a perfect job; she "worked" for the registry itself which *asked* if she was available for assignments. She no longer had to beg for days off and she could alter her schedule at any time if her circumstances changed.

Her assignments were short enough and varied enough so that she never had a chance to get bored working with the same nurses and doctors. On the other hand, if she really liked a place, she could usually manage to work there on a fairly regular basis.

As for the politics . . . as a registry nurse she was

not a part of the dirty pool that passed for interdepartmental relations.

An added bonus, one that she had not sought but surely welcomed, was the reduced workload that went along with being a "temporary." She was never assigned to the sickest patients, nor to patients under the care of perfectionist doctors.

The nursing office, in its infinite wisdom, knew that it was not cost effective to put a one-night nurse with a multi-complaint patient; it was just too hard to break into the patient care routine.

As for the doctors, the perfectionists among them liked to be able to lay blame. They liked to read the riot act and to throw tantrums. Their happiness depended on having the nurse "responsible" for any oversight or suspected error available for dressing down. Being told that they couldn't yell at the nurse because she'd only worked that one night made the doctors very, very irate.

The nursing office, as a matter of policy, liked to avoid irate doctors.

And she benefited from that; today she was taking care of a woman with migraine headaches, a man who had been hospitalized two days before with a total body sunburn, and an elderly woman admitted for observation after she'd fallen off her grandson's skateboard.

Not exactly a tough patient load.

The only problem, as she saw it, was the patient with the headaches, who rather doggedly persisted in asking, about every half hour, whether it was time yet for her medication.

It wasn't the asking that bothered Debbie; it was

the *way* in which she asked. Face scrunched up, voice trembling, hands shaking as if palsied, the woman deserved an Academy Award for best portrayal of a headache sufferer.

The woman had enough Demerol in her to bring an elephant to its knees, and she wanted more.

It was, thank God for both of them, almost time for the next shot.

Then she would go to lunch.

"Where in the world is the medication log?" Debbie looked up, expecting an answer. After all, she wasn't staff. But the nursing station was empty.

Not inclined to traipse around the halls looking for one of the regular nurses, she instead wrote the drug dose on a slip of paper and put it on top of the medication cart.

"Here's your medication, hon," she said as she entered the headache's room.

"Oh thank you."

The tears were a nice touch, Debbie thought, and slowly injected the drug through the IV line, watching the patient's eyelids as they began to droop.

Back at the station—it was still deserted—she was unable to find the chart.

"Great."

She wrote a second note with the time she'd given the drug and stuck it on a spindle near the phone; she would transfer the information to the chart when she got back from lunch.

"I'm going to lunch," she announced to anyone in hearing distance. She didn't really care whether they heard her or not.

Slathering mustard on her hot dog, she heard the code called over the intercom: "Code Blue to 318, Code Blue to 318."

She had bitten off a mouthful when she realized that 318 was the lady with the headache. Her patient was coding. Chewing the hot dog she contemplated going back to the floor and then decided against it. After all, everyone complained that pages were hard to hear in the cafeteria.

When she stepped off the elevator she had to stand aside for the hospital bed being pushed in.

It was her patient; one look at the lady's face and she knew that this was no performance.

"What happened?" she asked one of the other nurses after the elevator doors slid shut.

"Nobody knows," the nurse replied. "Kelly gave her the medication and she just stopped breathing."

Debbie jumped. "What?"

"The patient asked for her pain medication and according to the chart, she hadn't had any since eight a.m. So Kelly gave it to her and . . . maybe she had an allergic reaction to the Demerol or something."

"Or something."

When the excitement died down, Debbie found both of her notes and tore them up.

It wasn't really her fault, after all.

She went in to check on the man with the sunburn.

Chapter Forty-eight

"I'm sorry," Edana said, "whenever I hear them call a code, I keep expecting it to be Galen. And even when it's not, it makes me nervous."

Nervous was an understatement, Matt thought, watching her as she paced the room. When the intercom had blared its alarm she had looked at him with the frightened eyes of a skittish colt and the color had drained from her face.

"But he's off the respirator, you said."

"Maybe that's what I'm nervous about." Her smile was shaky. "At least on the respirator, I knew he'd keep breathing." She stopped by the window and looked out, hugging herself.

Matt wished that there was something he could do, but he was at a loss.

She looked at him as if sensing his dismay. "I'll be all right in a minute . . . I always am."

He hoped his smile was reassuring. "Maybe you'd feel better if you went in and saw him now."

She shook her head. "His grandfather's with him."

"I'm sure he'd understand." He crossed the room to stand by her side.

"He would, but it's better if I don't go in like this."

"What do you mean?" Studying her face, he noticed a delicate scar along her jaw line and he had to stop himself from reaching out to touch it.

"It's something I read once, years ago. There's a theory that children are born without fears, and that they only learn to be afraid by the reactions of others around them. A child falls down and his mother rushes to him, and he sees the worry on her face, and hears it in her voice, and he cries. Not from pain, but from fear . . . he picks up on her fears and makes them his own."

"Interesting theory."

She smiled. "I'm not sure they're wrong. When I was doing my clinical work there were a lot of times that patients—adult patients—would appear to be doing fine in every way from stable vital signs to a positive attitude. Then a well-meaning friend or family member would come in to cheer them up, and the next thing we knew, the patient was afraid for his life."

"And?"

"They're learning how fear can have a negative effect on patient outcome. There's been research that shows that the more positive the attitude, the better the outcome."

"But how could he pick up on it . . ."

"While he's in a coma? I don't know. But if you've worked around doctors and nurses for a while, sooner or later you'll hear about a coma patient who, when he or she woke up, was able to recount details about their treatment and even conversation they overheard while they were unconscious."

188

"That's spooky."

"Maybe . . . but if the unconscious mind can listen to words and sense what's happening to the body, it probably can also detect the emotional climate. And children are so much more aware of that kind of thing than adults are."

"I can't argue with that."

"Anyway, I'm calming down. See? My hands aren't even shaking anymore." She held out her hands.

His eyes were drawn to her wedding ring. He took her left hand in his, covering the gold band.

"Edana . . ."

She looked at him questioningly. "Yes?"

It's too early for this, he thought, and then leaned forward, kissing her lightly on the lips.

He took the stairs down to the ground level.

It was one-thirty and he was supposed to be back at the station.

He was not looking forward to this afternoon; the final reports on Galen Morgan had probably been typed by now, and he knew that he would need to tell Edana about her son very soon.

As much as he would hate doing it.

Procedure dictated that once the report was complete, his work was done unless he was required to testify in court. He was not obligated to tell her his conclusions, but he felt he had to. At some point she would need a copy of the police report for insurance purposes, and he didn't want her to find out that way.

It was important to him.

She was important to him.

The witness accounts were brutal. Hearing the details of the accident was disturbing enough; somehow it was worse to see them in black and white.

He particularly didn't want her to read the emotionless words that he himself had written without first understanding the constraints he was under to write a dispassionate report. He had to make her understand that he had no choice, he had to write what he suspected to be the truth no matter how he felt about the case personally.

And the truth was her boy had done it deliberately.

The witnesses said he looked straight at the car.

The witnesses said that in the split-second before the car hit him, he had smiled.

There was no doubt; too many people had seen it happen.

Edana, with a mother's eyes, may not have seen it the same way.

Soon he would have to tell her . . .

Waiting at an intersection for the light to change, he closed his eyes and saw her face and felt her lips beneath his.

She had smiled at him when he drew away, a smile that started deep in her eyes and ended in his soul.

He loved her, and he knew he could destroy her with a careless word.

Chapter Forty-nine

Becky made it to the hospital just as the clock showed 3:30 and heaved a sigh of relief.

"I'm here," she waved to the volunteer coordinator who peered over her glasses disapprovingly.

"You're not in uniform," the coordinator said.

"I will be. Back in two minutes."

Becky hurried down the hall to the employees' lounge and ducked inside, a little breathless from her mad dash across the hospital parking lot.

"Now I'm all sweaty," she said. She peeled her sweater off, wrinkling her nose in distaste. As she was stepping out of her skirt she noticed a big run in her nylons. "Great. Two ninety-five down the drain."

All because she had to rush to get here.

It was her mother's idea that she work as a candy-striper after school. "It'll be good for you . . . good experience." What mother meant and didn't say was: "It'll get you out of the house for a change."

Her father said it might help her get a job some day. What *he* meant and didn't say was: "You'll need to get a job because no man will ever marry you."

At sixteen, she had no friends, no dates, and no

prospects of getting any of either. Plus, she had no job.

She went to her locker and grabbed the pink-striped uniform and sighed. What kind of job would she be likely to get from sitting around looking like an obese candy cane?"

The zipper stuck halfway up and she struggled with it, cursing under her breath.

It was going to be just a dandy day.

She sat at the reception desk and watched people go by, making up stories for all of them. In her mind, the hospital was filled with intrigue, and every person had a secret to keep.

The guy in the Hawaiian shirt was a hit man, come to stop a government witness from testifying. The old couple standing in front of the gift shop were not married to each other; his wife was upstairs and soon they would go up and eliminate any need for a messy divorce. Another man in a blue suit only pretended to visit a friend; he was really a private investigator watching a married doctor making passes at the nurses. A teen-age girl had come to tell her boyfriend that the rabbit died.

Making up stories was the only thing that made the job tolerable.

Besides, it was good practice. When she grew up she was going to be a writer and she needed her imagination to be in top form.

"Becky."

Reluctantly she turned to look at the volunteer coordinator whose name she could never remember.

"Yes?" she asked politely.

"If you're not too busy," the woman said pointedly, her chins quivering, "I need you to go over to the dialysis unit and help them with discharges."

"Yes, ma'am."

The kidney dialysis unit was located all by itself, way down at the end of the ground floor hall.

Halls gave her the creeps ever since she had seen a movie where a crazy guy with an axe chased a voluptuous nurse down a deserted hallway just like this one. She kept expecting a door to open along the way and to feel the sting of cold metal slicing into her skull.

Did crazy men kill non-voluptuous teenagers?

She couldn't recall ever seeing a scene like that.

Maybe she was safe, she thought, and laughed nervously. Finally . . . something she was a natural at . . . repelling crazies.

She went up to the desk where two nurses were sitting, and waited patiently until they looked up to see what she wanted. "I'm supposed to help you with discharges?"

They exchanged a look.

"It'll be a few minutes," one of them said, "none of the patients are off the machine yet."

"Oh."

"Why don't you sit down and wait?" the other nurse suggested.

Becky could not think of anything she would want to do less, but there didn't seem to be a way out of it. "Okay."

The nurses resumed their conversation.

The machines fascinated her.

She knew from orientation that these patients came in several times a week to get their blood cleansed by the machines because their kidneys were no longer functioning.

She could actually see the blood going through clear tubes.

There were four patients—one man and three women—on the machine and they rested in lounge chairs—like her father had at home—and read magazines or watched TV; one of them was even asleep.

Becky *knew* that she could never sleep while her blood was being pumped out of her body.

None of them were paying any attention to her.

That suited her fine.

She perched on the edge of a chair and imagined that the machines were really some kind of vampire . . .

A high-tech Dracula.

She studied the face of the woman nearest her, trying to figure out what a vampire dialysis unit would put back into the patient. Something that just looked like blood, maybe, but then wouldn't the people die?

The woman stopped reading her magazine and used it to fan her face which was, Becky could see, becoming flushed.

Should she tell the nurses?

No; one of her mother's friends was about this lady's age, and she was forever complaining about hot flashes. That's what this looked like. It would only embarrass the woman if she drew attention to it.

The woman opened her mouth and began blowing as if trying to cool herself off. Then her hand went to her chest and she leaned forward in the lounge.

"Nurse?"

Becky turned quickly to see if the nurses had heard, but neither of them looked up.

When she looked back she saw that the other woman—this one much younger—was also looking very red in the face.

"Hello?" the first woman said. "I'm not feeling well."

Becky sprang to her feet and rushed to the desk. "I think they're getting sick."

She meant the two women, but in the space of time it took her to turn around, the others had begun to look bad as well.

"What in the . . ."

Just then an alarm went off at the first woman's bedside, and she sank back into the lounge, her face a violent purple.

"Get a doctor," one of the nurses yelled at her as they ran to the patients.

Becky grabbed the phone.

In two minutes the unit was swarming in nurses and doctors, and Becky stood with her back against the wall watching.

They moved the patients off the lounges and onto the floor so that they could do CPR. Working on their knees, desperation plain on their faces, they tried to breathe and pummel life back into dying bodies.

The doctors yelled orders at the nurses, and questions at each other, as if one of them might remember something the others had forgotten.

It went on for thirty minutes.

She began to cry as first one patient, and then the others, were declared dead.

The doctors stood around looking at each other in total disbelief.

Over and over, the rhyme ran through her head: "And all the king's horses, and all the king's men . . ."

She ran sobbing from the room.

Chapter Fifty

Kerri stood in the dark at the top of the stairs, listening to the voices from below.

Her grandfather had been talking almost steadily since just after dinner, trying to convince her mother to move the family to Iowa to live after Galen was out of the hospital.

"It'll be better for the kids," he said.

Mother's voice was softer, and Kerri had to strain to hear: "I understand how you feel, Dad, but . . ."

"You don't have to decide right now . . . think about it for a few days."

It was a moment before her mother spoke. "All right, I'll think about it, but . . ."

"It's a good place to live, honey, and I know you'd never be sorry."

"I'm not sure." Now her mother's tone was teasing. "Around December, when the snow is up around the rafters, I think I might miss the California sun."

"And the smog?" Grandpa laughed. "Would you miss that, too?"

"That isn't smog," Mother protested.

"No . . . just air you can cut with a knife."

The serious discussion was over, Kerri realized, and she moved silently along the hall toward her room.

Iowa.

Their mother had taken them to visit Grandpa on his farm even when they were babies, but the first time that Kerri really was aware was the year they were five.

Driving through the town, Grandpa had pointed out where a tornado had passed through. "Your dad was about seventeen," he'd said, and then he'd gotten very quiet.

Kerri looked out the window of the pick-up, curious to see what was different about a place a tornado had gone through, but if there was a difference, she didn't see it. She caught Galen watching her and stuck out her tongue.

"What was he like?" Galen asked.

"Your dad?" Grandpa looked at them with shiny eyes. "Well, he was a good boy, always helped out with the chores after he was old enough. Smart, too. Grandma and me knew by the time he was in second grade that we had to plan to send him to college."

Kerri yawned and looked out the window again, not listening to their talk.

Why talk about a man who died before she was born, even if he was her father?

The first thing she'd noticed about the farm was that there were no other houses close by. The house was set back from the main road in a grove of trees.

"To block the wind," Grandpa said when Galen asked what the trees were for. "See, here we don't

198

have a lot of hills and the wind sweeps on down."

Kerri didn't see *any* hills.

As for the wind, she couldn't imagine why anyone would not want the wind.

It blew her hair and pushed at her when she walked with her back to it, and the feel of it on her skin made her smile.

There was a small windmill that pumped water out of the ground, and it became her favorite place to be. She would lie underneath it, watching it spin, listening to the sound of the wind against the wooden blades.

But on the windiest days, Grandpa disconnected the pump to keep it from breaking apart, and on those days he made them stay in.

"You're too light," he said, "you'll blow away."

Kerri wanted desperately to find out if he was right, exulting inside at the thought of being pulled up into the air, a part of its energy.

Then there were the thunderstorms.

"This is nothing like you get in California," Grandpa promised, and it was true.

The night disappeared when lightning flashed, and for as long as it lasted you could see as clear and as bright as day. And the storms went on longer than any Kerri could remember from back home.

Once the blue-white flashes woke her in the middle of the night, and she tiptoed outside to stand under the violent sky. She had lifted her arms to the sky and then spun around for the sheer joy of it.

No one, not even Galen, understood her fascination.

No one saw the power that the wind and lightning

had over her.

She did not truly understand it herself, but she did not need to.

It was enough that she felt it.

Now she went to the window of her room and looked out on the dark night. The clouds had come back after yesterday's clear weather and they had blocked out the moon.

Not yet, Kerri knew; the storm was still building out at sea.

The power in her was building as well.

Within her, she knew, was the flow of the wind and the clash of thunder. Within her was the blinding light of power.

She spun in the silence of the room, creating her own wind, her bare feet moving across the cool wood floor. The window was open and the curtains began to flutter.

Eyes closed, head back, she felt the chill as it pervaded the room.

She laughed without sound.

WEDNESDAY

Chapter Fifty-one

Calvin waved at the bartender who was, he realized a little belatedly, standing only about a foot away.

"Can I have another?" He pointed at his empty glass.

"Can you tell time?" the bartender asked.

Calvin hated it when people answered a question with another question.

"I can. Now, can I have another drink?"

"Look around you, buddy, and tell me what you see."

He squinted. "What?"

"Look around."

Calvin swivelled on the bar stool and had to grab onto the counter to keep from falling. "Whoa." He swallowed because his mouth had suddenly filled with saliva, a good indication that he was about to be sick.

"Is there a bathroom here?"

The bartender sighed. "Over that way," he said, pointing into a dark corner of the room. A very dark, empty, corner.

Calvin lurched off the bar stool and walked quickly in that direction, determined not to show—or feel—

even the slightest bit of fear.

He was very surprised, when he got in the bathroom, to find it almost spotless. More surprised to notice the dispensers of certain female items on the lavender wall.

The lady's room.

A laugh escaped his lips, followed closely by the first rancid taste of beer.

When Calvin came out the bartender was standing in the middle of the room.

"Are you finished?" the bartender asked.

Chastened, Calvin nodded.

"Okay. Time to go home. Can you drive or do you want me to call you a cab."

"I walked," he lied. He had some pride left, even after puking all over the lady's room, and the ignominy of being driven to his door like some kind of pathetic drunk did not appeal to him in the least.

"Do you live far from here?"

Calvin shook his head, although he wasn't really sure where "here" was. "I'll walk."

"Suit yourself."

Outside, Calvin took a deep breath, filling his lungs with air and trying to rid himself of the stench of beer. He supposed that vomiting until it came out his nostrils had something to do with the persistence of the smell.

"Well, good night, and good luck."

He watched as the bartender got into a sportylooking car and drove off without a backward glance.

When he was certain that he was alone in the

parking lot, he walked quickly to his own car and got the key in the door on the second try. Inside, he locked the door and sat behind the wheel, shivering.

Should he try to drive home?

He didn't feel drunk anymore, but with his limited experience he thought it was possible that he could still be drunk and not know it.

Working at the hospital, he had seen too many victims of drunk drivers to want to try it himself. There was no way, after the close call with the Death Committee, that he wanted another accident on his conscience.

He maneuvered himself until his legs were on the front seat, his feet propped against the passenger door. With his head against the cool glass, he fell asleep.

Someone was tapping on the window.

For a moment he thought he was home on the couch, and when he tried to swing his legs to the floor, he hit the dashboard with his knee.

He opened his mouth to swear and then noticed the familiar and unmistakable silhouette of a police car parked a few feet away.

He rolled down the window. "Hello, officer."

"You having trouble?"

"No . . . no, I just had a little too much to drink and I thought I'd better sleep it off." The words, he was relieved to hear, sounded coherent.

"Good idea, but this is a bad neighborhood to be caught dozing in . . . why don't I give you a lift home."

Calvin nodded slowly. Pride be damned; his entire body ached, for some reason, and going home to sleep in his own bed was the only sensible thing to do.

He locked up his car and limped—his right leg had gone to sleep—to the patrol car.

There were only a few other cars on the street and all of them were driving slowly.

"Either they're drunk," the cop said, "or they've seen me."

"Don't the drunks see you too?"

The cop laughed. "The drunks don't see anything . . . Patton could land the troops on Harbor Boulevard and the drunks would miss it."

Calvin laughed politely.

"So," the cop said, "which way?"

"What?"

"Where do you live?"

"Where are we now?"

The cop cast him a sideways glance. "It's a very good thing you aren't driving . . ."

"I don't know where I am a lot of the time when I'm sober," Calvin said honestly, and then recited his address.

"I don't need the zip code."

"Sorry." As he turned his head to look out, he noticed a car speeding toward the intersection they were about to enter. "Uh . . . sir?"

It happened so fast that the policeman didn't have a chance to react.

The other car hit the front end of the patrol car with enough force to turn them in at a ninety degree angle before continuing on to slam into a traffic standard.

Calvin knew this was a dream.

A vivid dream, but there was no other reasonable explanation for what happened next.

He could see, turning his head carefully, three other intersections, north, south, and east. Within seconds of the time the patrol car came to rest, he watched as cars crashed, with varying degrees of force, in all three directions.

The policeman, who in his dream had started to run across to the car wrapped around the pole, stopped in the center of the road.

In the seconds before the dream ended, Calvin saw that all of the traffic lights, in every direction, were blinking green.

Everyone had the right of way.

Chapter Fifty-two

Dave Levine sat at the desk in the emergency room, working a crossword puzzle while waiting for the white count on a patient he suspected might have appendicitis.

"What's a six letter word meaning 'sloth'," he asked.

"Doctor."

"What?"

"Doctor is a six letter word meaning sloth," the nurse said, and smiled.

"Very funny." He looked back at the puzzle, but it was obvious the word wouldn't fit. "Respect for me aside, you should never joke about something as serious as a crossword . . ."

She held up her hand to silence him. "Listen."

He listened and then shook his head. "I don't . . ."

"Sirens." She got up and started toward the ambulance doors. "A lot of them."

Then he could hear them too, and he followed her out to stand in the ambulance bay.

"A fire maybe?" There seemed to be too many of them for anything else, unless it was a major disaster of some sort, but if it were a disaster, they would have been notified by now on the HEAR radio.

"I don't know," the nurse said, "but I don't like the sound of it."

They looked at each other.

Behind them, the red emergency phone began to ring.

Dave stood beside her, reading the notes she was taking as she listened to the dispatcher on the phone.

T.C. meant traffic collision, he knew, and he could decipher all of the medical information—none of which indicated serious or life-threatening injuries—but the very number of victims listed seemed catastrophic.

"Yes," she was saying, "thanks." She hung up the phone.

"You thanked them for that?" The list of victims covered most of a page. "They do know that there are other hospitals in the area . . ."

"It's the same everywhere," she said, edging past him and going straight to a department phone. She picked up the receiver and punched the O for operator.

"What?"

"I don't know, Dr. Levine, the dispatcher wasn't specific, but I gather there've been accidents all over the country." Then she spoke into the phone. "Emergency room standby."

The terse order was relayed a scant second later over the intercom: "Emergency room standby to the emergency room, emergency room standby to the emergency room . . . please."

"Please," he muttered under his breath. "Everyone's so damned polite."

In ten minutes there was not an empty bed left.

Dave worked as quickly as he could, moving from one patient to the next, triaging them according to severity of injury.

None of them looked too bad—a few cuts, a lot of contusions, a possible broken bone or two—but he always treated trauma patients as potential fatalities, even if they were sitting up and joking with each other. It was not catastrophic, as he had feared, it was more like . . . a carnival.

The hard part was getting some of the jokers to take him seriously.

"I'm fine," one of them laughed, "why don't you go take a look at my car, see if you can do anything for it?"

Dave understood clearly why so many of them were "fine": the fumes of alcohol being breathed out were beginning to make *him* a little dizzy.

He didn't want to resort to scare tactics, but by the time three patients had grabbed his stethoscope and shouted into it, he knew there was no alternative.

"Listen, you guys," he said, standing in the center of the room and pulling himself up to his full height, "I've seen people come in here looking better than any of you who dropped dead an hour later because they were 'fine' and didn't need any medical help. Far be it for me to infringe upon your rights to bleed to death in the privacy of your own homes. But let me say this . . ." He looked at the faces around him. "I'm going to write on your charts 'refused medical treatment,' and I'm going to get it witnessed by the nurses and some of these policemen here, and when your family tries to sue us, so that they can live high on the hog as a result of your deaths, they'll be clean out of luck."

Someone laughed and then they all started up again.

Dave turned and stalked away.

He knew his failure to intimidate them was because he wasn't tall.

By six a.m. the emergency room was empty again.

One patient, who by coincidence worked at the hospital, had been admitted for observation for a possible concussion. Hall was the name.

The rest, a little more sober after the police lab technician had come to draw blood alcohol levels on all of them, left under their own power as relatives and friends drifted in to claim them.

No one had collapsed and died.

Dave sat with his feet up on the desk and resumed work on his crossword puzzle.

"What's a six letter word for tantrum?"

"Levine," the nurse suggested, looking at him innocently.

He paused. "You know, we're really lucky someone wasn't killed."

"Yeah . . . you."

Scowling, he looked back at the puzzle.

The red phone rang again.

Chapter Fifty-three

Agatha always arrived early at the hospital for her shift at the information desk. As the head volunteer, director of all the pink ladies, she thought it behooved her to set a good example for the others. And, she admitted to herself, it got her away from home where Chester's ghost tended to haunt her in the early morning hours.

"Breakfast ready yet?" she'd hear him ask, but of course he was never really there. She just imagined it.

Other things that she imagined which were never really there included the sound of his footsteps, the smell of his pipe, and the creak of the rocker on the porch.

She had loved Chester dearly when he was alive, but she thought it a little unfair that he would give her no peace.

"I wouldn't do this to you," she'd chirp when she thought he might be in the room.

The pipe smoke in particular was annoying; it got so bad sometimes that she had to spray rose-scented air freshener around the room.

Well, at least he'd never followed her when she went

out . . . so far, anyway.

"Morning," she called, and wiggled her fingers in greeting at Hank, the security guard.

He lifted a hand in salute and then, baton swinging impressively from his hip, walked down the hall.

Agatha watched after him; she'd always liked a man in uniform. Sighing, she went to the information desk and sat down behind it, unlocking the drawers and pulling out the necessary supplies for the day.

Pencils, a pad of paper, a stapler and a card file. The census sheet had been left in the in-basket, along with the schedule of admissions.

Not many admissions, she saw.

Her job was to direct visitors to the correct patient rooms and to direct the new admits to admitting. She also kept a card file of recent discharges so that she could forward any late mail they received to their homes.

The front doors opened and the morning shift began to arrive.

"Another day, another dollar," she called out cheerfully to each group that passed.

Some waved and some just made faces, but she made certain that all of them heard.

When all but the tardy had passed through the lobby, she dug through the desk for the schedule.

Justine was scheduled to come in at eight.

Agatha frowned. Justine was nice enough, she supposed, but the woman had made an art form out of applying fingernail polish, and it was *very* annoying to sit at the desk with her and watch stroke after stroke of polish being applied.

It also smelled.

She should have brought the air freshener from home.

"Well," she said to herself, closing the drawer emphatically, "I'll just have to make my rounds last a little longer than usual today."

When Justine was safely ensconced at the desk, Agatha announced that she was on her way.

"Sure," Justine nodded, not missing a stroke.

Agatha could not stop herself from sniffing and wrinkling her nose. "That stuff really smells, Justine."

"Does it?" Unperturbed, Justine smiled. "It won't when it's dry."

When would it ever get a chance to dry, Agatha wondered, but she knew it was pointless to comment any further. "Ta ta," she said, and started off down the hall.

As luck would have it, Hank had already gone off-shift and the guard in his place looked at her stupidly when she peeked around the corner at him.

"Oh, I thought you were someone else."

The guard snapped his gum. "Happens all the time."

Agatha hadn't the faintest idea what he was talking about, but neither did she care.

"Ta ta."

Well, she'd see Hank another time.

Hank was one of the reasons that she wished Chester would evaporate, or whatever it was that ghosts did. She very much wanted to ask Hank to dinner, but she was afraid of what might happen— what Chester might do—if she did.

Chester had always been a little on the jealous side.

Not that he'd had cause when he was alive; she was a devoted wife who had never even been tempted by the attentions of another man.

But now that he was dead . . .

Well, she still had a little spring in her step, a little fire in the chimney. And Chester's ghost, for all his inventiveness, could not stoke that fire.

Hank, she suspected, might.

The only problem was, what if she invited Hank to dinner and Chester did something . . . ghostly?

She'd seen *Poltergeist*, she knew what that might mean.

She just couldn't take a chance like that. What if some of that jello-looking protoplasm dropped onto the table while they were eating dinner, for God's sake.

No, sir.

And she didn't have it in her, not at her age, to invite herself over to Hank's house to cook.

Liberation, as far as she was concerned, was what happened to France when the allied armies arrived.

Maybe she could move out of the house, buy a condo . . .

In E.R. she stopped to chat for a while with the nurses. While she talked she kept an eye on the patients, always waiting for one of them to take a turn for the worst. Felice, one of the other volunteers, had been witness once to a heart attack, and she had regaled them for weeks with what she had seen.

Agatha, as director, didn't like to be outdone.

"What's wrong with him?" She pointed at a young

man, his jean legs cut almost up to his private parts, who was on the first gurney. He was scraped up and had a nasty cut on his forehead, but otherwise appeared alert.

"Motorcycle accident . . . waiting for x-rays."

"He doesn't look too bad." She hoped that her disappointment didn't show.

"He was lucky," the nurse said, "but he doesn't know it."

"How do you mean?"

"He says the first thing he's gonna do when he gets out of here is get back on his bike . . . I guess some people just never learn."

Agatha agreed.

A few minutes later, the young man started gasping for air, and Agatha turned hopefully toward the nurse.

"He's hyperventilating again," the nurse shrugged, "he's been doing that every ten minutes or so since he got here." She went over to the bedside and handed him a paper bag. In a minute he began to relax.

"Okay," the nurse said, "let me just give you a little oxygen so you'll know that you're breathing okay." She slipped a green-tinted plastic mask over his nose and mouth. "There you go."

Agatha had come up to the gurney and she looked down at the young man with her warmest smile.

"He wants me to hold his hand, I think," the nurse said.

"I'll stay with him for a bit," Agatha offered. Maybe he would start to hyperventilate again while she was there; it would be better than nothing.

After the nurse left she noticed that his eyelids

seemed to be drooping a bit.

"Need more air?" she asked cheerfully.

There was no response.

She looked around for the nurse again, didn't see her, and then decided she could do it herself. She had her first aid certificate, after all.

Reaching for the valve on the portable oxygen canister, she hesitated, vaguely troubled.

There was something different about the oxygen tank.

Agatha studied it.

What was it, though?

Leaning over, she touched the cool metal surface. Wasn't it supposed to be a green tank? There was lettering on it, so she turned it until the words faced up.

Nitrous oxide.

Agatha gasped and jumped up, pulling the mask from the young man's face and slapping him soundly on both cheeks.

"Nurse!" she yelled, "Doctor!"

Chapter Fifty-four

John wandered through the house, a mug of coffee in his hand, looking at Edana's furniture and trying to imagine it in his house. It would take a bit of doing, to fit it all in, but he thought he could manage.

Having someone else at the house would take a little getting used to, after six and a half years of being alone, but that he was looking forward to. He definitely would welcome a little more noise in that quiet place.

He stopped at one of the front windows and pulled the curtain aside, looking out at the street. A crew from the city had finally come by to fix all the street lights, and they were almost finished.

City crews would be hopping today, unless he missed his guess. The morning radio said that every traffic signal in a five mile radius was on the blink, and cops were directing traffic.

Cops.

He wondered if Garrett was right when he suggested that the cop—what was his name?—was in pursuit of Edana. Edana's evasive response to Garrett's teasing could mean anything.

The last thing Edana needed, in his opinion, was to get involved with a man in such a dangerous line of work. Being widowed twice was not what he wanted for her.

"Hell," he said, "they only met a few days ago."

But that didn't make him feel any better; he had known about Mary—that she was the one—the moment he'd laid eyes on her. And he'd been as persistent a suitor as ever was born.

If the cop was like that, Edana wouldn't be moving to Iowa, now or any other time.

He let the curtain drop and turned away.

With just him in it, this house was as lonely as his own.

He had sent Edana on to the hospital by herself this morning by claiming to be a little under the weather, and then watched Kerri walk off to school. What he'd planned, the night before, was to start calling around to moving companies. He'd thought if he had all the facts and figures, he could make a more convincing argument when they talked again.

By the time an hour had passed, however, he knew he couldn't do it. After some hard thinking, he knew it wouldn't be right to go behind her back like that.

Maybe he was getting soft in his old age. Or maybe part of him knew that, whatever he did, it wasn't going to happen. Part of him knew that maybe it *shouldn't* happen.

That knowledge had come upon him gradually, as he went from room to room, and became aware of something he hadn't noticed before.

The house had a settled feeling, a feeling of permanence.

This was the home that Galen was going to come home to.

And the boy had a right to come back to the only home he had ever known.

John felt a catch in his throat, and he knew he had to love them all enough to let them be. If Edana could find someone else who made her happy, he had to give his blessings and stand aside.

He had had his life, and now he had to let them have theirs.

Chapter Fifty-five

Megan came up beside the nurse who was just finishing taking Galen's blood pressure.

"How is he this morning?" she asked.

"About the same . . . his temperature is back to normal, respiration is unlabored."

"He hasn't shown any signs of needing the respirator?"

"Not a one."

"Good." Megan touched her hand to the boy's face. "Galen, can you hear me?"

He didn't move.

"A little while ago," the nurse said, putting the blood pressure cuff back in the holder, "somebody dropped a metal basin, and I thought I saw him jump a little."

"Really . . . that's good." She brushed the hair back from his forehead. "When he's ready, I think he'll just wake up and surprise us all."

"Dr. Turner," a voice called from behind her.

She turned to see one of the police officers she had spoken with on Monday hurrying toward her. The one who had given her the card for Edana Morgan

. . . Kennedy, that was the name.

"Yes?"

"Do you have a minute to talk to me? About Galen Morgan?"

She glanced at her watch; administration had called an emergency meeting of all available doctors and nurses for eleven a.m., and it was a quarter to. "A few minutes," she said.

"Is there somewhere we can talk privately?"

"We can try the doctor's lounge."

There was no one in the lounge and Megan closed the door, turning to face Officer Kennedy.

"I think you should know," the officer began, "that the official police report concludes that Galen Morgan stepped in front of the car deliberately the night he was hit."

Megan frowned. "When you say 'concludes,' what do you mean? There's no doubt?"

"Very little doubt."

"I see. And what led you to that conclusion?"

"There were several witnesses, besides the boy's mother, and their statements are essentially identical. With a few minor differences, every one of the witnesses saw the same thing."

"What differences?"

"Subjective differences of perception about some of the details . . ."

"I'm sorry, I'm not following you."

"Well, the car was described as tan by one witness, and pale yellow by another . . . that type of thing. What I mean is, none of the differences cast any doubt on the truth of the overall statements."

Megan was silent, assimilating what Kennedy had told her. "And they all were able to say positively that it was a deliberate act on Galen's part? How could they know that?"

"There was just no doubt that the boy saw the car coming at him. The driver of the car says that they made eye contact, and the boy smiled at him. He naturally assumed that Galen would stay where he was, at the curb, and so he didn't slow down. The witnesses were positioned on almost every side of where Galen was standing, and they all said that Galen *had* to have seen the car. They saw him smile, and they saw him step in front of the car and wait for it to hit him. He never even flinched, from what they said."

"Oh God."

"I know, it's hard to believe, a seven year old . . ."

"Well, seven is sometimes called 'the age of discretion,' and kids are attempting suicide at that age, and younger, but stepping in front of a car is a rather brutal way to go about it."

"Brutal for everyone concerned."

She looked at him. "Yes, I imagine it is."

Kennedy hesitated. "Mrs. Morgan doesn't know yet . . . about the report conclusions."

"She witnessed it, I thought."

"She did, but from her angle she wouldn't have seen . . . or at least I don't think she would have seen . . . what made the witnesses so sure that it was an intentional act . . . Galen smiling at the driver."

"And she doesn't have any suspicions."

Again, that hesitation. "She might have her suspi-

cions . . . when she gave her statement, she said."
Kennedy closed his eyes, reciting from memory: "*He went to the curb and stopped there. Then he turned and yelled 'no' again, and he stepped off the curb, right in front of the car.*"

"He yelled no? Do you know what that was about?"

"His mother said he'd been having an argument with his sister, and he ran out of the house."

"I see." How did the sister feel about that, Megan wondered.

"Anyway, what I really am trying to do, is ask your advice about telling Edana . . . Mrs. Morgan."

"Yes, well I can see how that might be difficult, if she really hasn't come to that conclusion on her own."

"Do you think it's possible she has? Come to the same conclusion?"

Megan shook her head. "I've talked to her daily, and I think she would tell me anything that she thought might have a bearing on Galen's recovery. And a suicide attempt is always a factor to take into account . . ." She studied Kennedy's face. "I'll tell her, if you want me to."

"No . . . I have to do it," he said, "it has to be me."

"Then my only advice to you is to see if you can help her come to a conclusion of her own."

"How?"

"Have her tell you again, and ask her what she thinks it all means. Ask how she feels. I think she's a very intuitive person, and if she examines her memories of the accident, she'll know what it means. He's

224

her son and she knows him better than anyone else could possibly know him."

Except, Megan thought, his twin sister.

Chapter Fifty-six

"Hey, are you coming?"

Sharon looked up to see Randi at the door. "In just a minute, as soon as I finish this."

"You don't want to be late, you know; Nolan's on the war path and he might just jump down your throat if you come in after he's started."

"Well," Sharon said, "he can jump ahead . . . he doesn't frighten me."

"Famous last words."

Sharon laughed. "Go on, coward, and save me a seat."

"Hot seat." Randi disappeared around the door, calling out behind her: "Hurry."

"Easier said than done," and looked back at the mess on the bedside utility tray.

The patient had stomach cancer and was being fed via a hyperalimentation line. The catheter was threaded through his internal jugular vein for infusion of the hypertonic solution into the superior vena cava.

It was only the second time she'd ever worked with a patient on hyperalimentation, and she had carefully reviewed the procedures manual to refresh her memory. She had also watched one of the other nurses do it this morning, and she felt reasonably confident that she was prepared.

She just didn't want to be rushed.

The patient wasn't rushing her, that was for certain; he was totally out of it. Eighty-two years old and you'd think they'd let him die in peace, but he was caught up in the system, and if his veins closed down from too many IVs they'd plug the joy juice right into his heart.

Even as a nurse, she found the medical profession's reluctance to let go before the last trick was turned morally repugnant.

It was a dirty rotten shame.

"Well," she said to him, "doctor's orders."

She realized immediately what she had done: an air bubble—a big one—was in the line, moving toward the base of the catheter.

When it reached the patient's heart, it would kill him.

She had only seconds to think.

Hands shaking, she began pulling the heart monitor leads out of the electrodes so that there would be no tracings of the event, and then spun to silence the cardiac alarm by hitting the reset button.

Then she stood back and made herself watch.

When his body was still she re-attached the monitor which showed a straight line.

She walked slowly from the room and went to the

nursing station where she picked up the phone to notify the patient's doctor.

"It was fast," she said, when the doctor asked.

That, at least, was the truth.

Chapter Fifty-seven

Willie sat at the back of the auditorium, listening as Terence Nolan began to read through the list of events that he was terming 'incidents.'

"The first report covers a computer malfunction in ICU on Saturday morning. When I first reviewed this report, I mistakenly placed it in a no-injury file. Mistakenly because the nurse who filled it out made no reference . . . *no reference at all*, to the fact that within minutes after the computer failed, two patients died in ICU."

He paused and looked around the room. "I agree, at first glance, that the malfunction and the patient deaths would not appear to be related. And in fact, I have been informed that a satisfactory cause of death was established in both cases. However, I cannot stress enough how crucial it is that every incident report be as complete and accurate as possible, because if this mechanical problem *had contributed* to those deaths, our investigation would have been seriously compromised by such careless reporting."

"Now," he continued after a moment, "that same day we had several relatively minor, non-injury incidents which nonetheless would seem to suggest that something is going on here."

Willie frowned. Was he, she wondered, suggesting that someone was intentionally doing these things?

"Then there was the scare with the fire alarms early Monday morning . . . I shouldn't have to tell you that it was a potentially dangerous situation, and we were just lucky that none of the patients had a heart attack or that no one was caught in the fire doors when they closed."

Willie took a deep breath; she knew what was next on the list.

Nolan held a hand up and called for silence. "The next incident, I'm sorry to say, resulted in a fatality. A patient on the medical floor was given an overdose of morphine. I have read this report through time and again, and there is no doubt in my mind that the nurse involved was at fault."

She had expected that conclusion, but expecting it didn't make hearing it any easier.

"There was, that same morning, a patient who was asphyxiated in surgery . . ." Nolan paused, ". . . by a machine malfunction."

Willie felt the blood rush to her face. That was an outright lie. Every one of the surgery nurses knew that it was the anesthesiologist who was to blame for that death. But she kept quiet, wanting to hear what else Nolan had to say.

"On Tuesday we had a second overdose . . . the details on that incident have not yet revealed a clearcut picture of what happened . . . and then, as I'm sure all of you know, there were the dialysis deaths . . . let me read from this." He cleared his throat.

" 'Dialyzer examined and was found to have a faulty heating unit, resulting in the over-warming of blood. In addition, the blood may have been diluted.' "

"Oh no," Willie whispered. She had read about a similar case back east; the patients died of hemolysis as the red blood cells essentially burst from the heat.

"And the last case—as far as we know—was a patient in E.R. who received nitrous oxide instead of oxygen. Thankfully, he was not seriously injured."

A murmur rose in the room and again Nolan held up his hand.

"There are two other events that I know you all have heard about . . . Dr. Abrahms' death and the helicopter crash. Both are police cases, and I am not at liberty to divulge any information as to their current status or disposition. But I will say the police are actively pursuing the parties responsible and both investigations are ongoing." He frowned, pensive.

"Yesterday, I had the opportunity to talk to several of you about these incidents, and it was suggested to me that many, if not most of them, might be acts of sabotage."

Willie could not believe what she was hearing.

"So my question to you is, who, in this hospital, is capable of such acts?"

She pushed through the auditorium doors and walked quickly down the hall.

"Willie," a voice called out.

"Ray, what are you doing here?"

"The fire department goes where it is sent," he said, catching up to her and walking at her side.

231

"Speaking of fires, you look like you're a little 'het up,' as my dad used to say."

"More than a little."

"So what's wrong."

Willie stopped suddenly and faced him as other people passed them in the hall.

"You ever caught a lizard, Ray?"

He laughed, uncertain. "A lizard? What's that . . ."

"Got to do with it? Everything. The first thing a kid learns about a lizard is not to catch it by the tail, 'cause the lizard is built so that it can lose its tail, and do just fine."

"So?"

"Nurses are the lizard's tail of a hospital. The hospital can always sacrifice a nurse or two if trouble happens, and then it does just fine, too."

Ray frowned. "What's going on?"

"I've told you about some of the things that have been happening here . . ."

He nodded. "And?"

"Nolan's looking to find someone he can sacrifice to save the hospital." She noticed she was drawing some strange looks from a few of the doctors as they passed by. "Gotta save the hospital at all costs," she said savagely, not caring who heard her. "You know what they're going to call the new building they're planning? The Tower, like it was some citadel . . . or something holy. There's nothing holy about this place."

Ray put his arm around her shoulder and guided her down the hall. "Come on, Willie, let's get out of here."

232

He walked with her to where her car was parked and held her tightly.

"You're shaking," he said.

"I can't help it . . . I'm so mad."

"I don't blame you, but think of the way in which you can do the most good here . . ."

"Oh, Ray, I don't know what to think. I want to go in there and quit. Join the Peace Corp. Join the Foreign Legion. Just anything to get away from . . . from that!"

"He's one man," Ray said.

"But there are others who feel the same way he does. I saw heads nodding while he was talking. I know some bad things have been happening, but you just don't throw the baby out with the bath water. What he's doing is turning us on each other. Nobody's going to be able to make a move without ten other people watching them. I can't work like that."

"Hush." He lifted her chin and kissed her. "Go home and try to rest . . . you've got to work tonight."

She tried to relax. "Can you come in with me and watch my back?"

"Baby, nobody is out to get you."

"I wonder," she said.

Chapter Fifty-eight

Irma Jean stood back in the shadows, looking through the screen door at the apartment across the way, trying to decide if, as manager of the complex, she should take a little peek inside. The tenant hadn't showed his face in a while, and his car wasn't in the carport, so she was reasonably sure he wasn't around.

What had caught her attention was what had happened the other day, when the phone had been ringing off the hook and she *knew* he was home to answer it.

She was more than a little suspicious about that.

Was he trying to avoid someone? Like creditors, maybe? If so, there was a distinct possibility that he might try to skip on his rent.

It was always tricky, going in an apartment while the tenant wasn't there, but in the middle of the day, at least, it wasn't too likely that anyone would see her.

The only problem was that he kept strange hours.

He worked at West Valley Hospital, she knew, mostly days but sometimes evenings. There was a chance he might come home while she was prowling . . . looking around.

But it was her job, after all, to keep an eye on things. And if he had nothing to hide, he shouldn't mind . . .

That decided it; she had to do her duty.

Inserting the key into the deadbolt, she glanced one last time over her shoulder to see if anyone was coming into the courtyard, then twisted the key and pushed the door open in a rush.

She breathed a little easier when she was on the inside with the door between her and any watchful eyes.

"Phew," she said, grimacing. Something smelled bad. She had a sudden thought about bodies decomposing, but Hall had never had anyone to the apartment in all of the time he'd been living here, so it wasn't too likely that he'd done a girl friend in, or anything.

The smell turned out to be just ripening garbage in the kitchen. A health hazard, maybe, but not a felony.

The bedroom was where she went next, curious whether she'd find the usual male substitutes for female company. Pornography, they called it on TV; she called it smut.

Trusting her experience of some thirty-one years as a married woman, she checked under the bed, but all she found were assorted dirty articles of clothing and about a cubic ton of dust.

He had been living here for quite a long time.

She got up off her knees, put her hands on her hips, and turned a slow circle, surveying the room through narrowed eyes.

In a drawer somewhere?

She nodded grimly, and set about her search.

By the time she had been through the bedroom, bathroom and living room, she was beginning to think she might have been wrong about Hall. All she had found were computer magazines. Well-worn computer magazines, with nary a naked thigh in sight.

"Sick," she said, and slumped on the couch, her chin in her hand.

She didn't know what to make of Calvin Hall.

"The kitchen," she said. With the exception of the garbage can, the kitchen was virgin territory; she hadn't checked those drawers and cabinets.

She'd never heard of a man keeping his smut in the kitchen, but Hall was no ordinary man, she was sure.

Eagerly she got up from the couch, visualizing a stack of magazines hidden behind boxes of cereal. If she found them, she would take them. Let him hunt all day and all night for that disgusting, filthy trash.

She would laugh at him from her place of watching.

In her fervor to find the pictures, she almost missed it, lying in plain view on the kitchen table.

A note.

I killed them. It was an accident, the note read.

Irma Jean knew immediately what it was; a confession. She wasn't sure who the 'them' was, since she only knew of the one murder, that of the doctor, but the police would know.

Chapter Fifty-nine

Rita turned the television on for company and then went into the kitchen to fix something to eat, hungry for the first time in days.

She felt decidedly better since the call had come from the hospital, asking her to work tonight. The relief nurse had called in sick, according to the staffing secretary, who then went on to imply that a suspiciously high number of nurses had suddenly taken ill after a meeting of some sort with administration.

Rita didn't care about any of that; she never attended meetings scheduled during her time off, and whatever that double-dealer Nolan had to say didn't interest her.

All that mattered was that she would be able to take care of Galen Morgan. If the unit was short-handed because of a case of the "white flu," she might be assigned another patient or two, but she would take care of them in short order.

The weatherman was saying that the thunderstorms he'd been predicting for the past few days were moving in from the sea. "Batten down your hatches," he said, making it sound like an adventure.

Rita looked across the breakfast bar at the set to watch as the radar showed the progression of the storm over the past twenty-four hours.

Good. She wouldn't have to wash the car.

From the corner of her eye she saw a familiar face on the screen.

". . . are questioning a suspect in the death of prominent Orange Country neurosurgeon, Samuel Abrahms," the announcer said, and Abrahms' picture was replaced by footage showing an outside view of the hospital.

Rita moved around the counter.

"Abrahms was killed," the announcer continued, "at West Valley Hospital, sometime early Saturday morning. An exact cause of death has not been released by the coroner's office and police officials refused tonight to reveal the name of the suspect. An anonymous source, however, indicated that the suspect was an employee at West Valley, and that much, at least, has been confirmed at this time."

"Hmm." Someone working at the hospital, most likely, she thought, someone on the graveyard shift. "It figures."

However closed-mouth the police were being, she knew very well that every person working tonight would know who the police were questioning.

And there was, for her, a perverse pleasure in knowing something that the all-mighty media didn't: since shortly after Abrahms' body was found, the cause of death was common knowledge among the staff.

Someone had drilled into his skull and aspirated

his brain.

The question they all had, though, was how?

She left the apartment at six and the wind had picked up enough to wrap her coat tightly around her legs. The clouds were dark and angry-looking, but it hadn't yet started to rain.

Chapter Sixty

Megan sat at the nurse's station, finishing her continuation notes on Galen Morgan.

His condition had remained essentially the same since he had been taken off the respirator, with only minimal indications of increased awareness. While he had reportedly reacted to a sudden loud noise earlier, there was no response to spoken commands.

The neurological exam, according to Dr. Stafford's notes, showed marginal improvement.

Galen seemed to be at equilibrium.

His mother and grandfather had been in, as usual, after dinner, and she had talked with them briefly. Apparently the police officer, Kennedy, had not yet spoken to Edana Morgan, because she was in good spirits, optimistic that as each day passed, Galen was closer to waking up.

The grandfather was a little more guarded, Megan thought, but more than that he was annoyed that he had come all the way to California to catch a cold.

"Do you know how cold it is in Iowa this time of

year?" he'd asked, and both she and Edana had laughed at his indignation.

Watching Edana with Galen, Megan did not envy Kennedy the task of having to suggest that the boy had brought this all on himself. But she also thought that Edana had strengthened in the past five days, and that she would be able to handle anything, as long as her son was alive.

The Morgans had left early—the grandfather just a little pale—after she had assured them the hospital would call if there were any changes in the child's condition.

She closed the chart and looked across the room at him, his small form absolutely still.

"What do you think, Dr. Turner?"

The nurses, who had been holding quiet but intense discussion ever since she'd arrived, were looking at her.

"I'm sorry, I haven't been listening."

"Do you think one person could have done all the things that Nolan was talking about?"

Megan had heard the speculation that the man the police were questioning in connection with Abrahms' death was considered something of a mechanical genius, who would have had the knowledge required to tamper with the dialysis machine as well as almost every piece of equipment in the hospital.

"Maybe," she said after a moment, "but I'd think someone would have seen something sooner or later. Or seen him, if it was him."

"But everything fits," one of them said. "He

241

worked here, so he had access to all of the equipment. All he would have to do was sneak in when no one was around . . . there's hardly a place in this hospital that isn't deserted at least some of the time."

"That's right," a second nurse agreed. "The dialysis unit is only open during the day, the surgery schedule starts at seven in the morning . . ."

"And even when there are emergency surgeries at night," the first nurse interrupted, "they usually only use one of the rooms, and the rest are empty."

"As for the elevators and all that other stuff, if you know what you're doing . . . and Calvin is a whiz with that kind of thing . . . it would only take a few minutes to mess up the machinery."

"I can see what you're getting at," Megan said, "but what about the overdoses?"

"In the first one, what Nolan didn't mention was that the nurse had to leave the room for a minute to get a box of syringes. Anyone could have come in and substituted a vial of morphine for the Demerol."

"Morphine is kept under lock and key," Megan reminded them.

"A lock wouldn't be much of a challenge for someone like Calvin. And that second overdose, no one knows who gave the patient the first injection . . ."

"And he'd been acting strangely . . ." one of the others contributed. "Sneaking around in the middle of the night, fussing with the computer, and looking, to be honest, as guilty as hell about *something*."

"He didn't show up for work all week."

"Well, *that* I don't blame him for," a voice said firmly.

Megan frowned. "I think it's better not to jump to conclusions. From what I heard on the news, the police are only questioning him. They haven't arrested him yet."

Chapter Sixty-one

Edana opened the door, a smile on her face, but instead of Jeff, coming back for one last word, it was Matt Kennedy standing on the porch.

"Oh," she said, startled. "I thought you were someone else."

"I know, I saw him drive away."

"Pardon?"

"Your friend with the Porsche . . . I was parked across the street and I waited until he left . . ."

She was confused. "You've been waiting across the street for Jeff to leave? But why?"

"I wanted to talk to you in private . . ."

"He's a good friend," she said, still not understanding.

"Do you mind if I come in?"

"No . . . of course not." She unlatched the screen door and pushed it open. "Is it about Galen?"

He nodded and held out a manila envelope. "I brought you the police reports."

She started to reach for them and then stopped. Something in his expression seemed foreboding.

"Come and sit down," she said, dropping her hand to her side. She turned and walked ahead of him into the living room.

"First," he said, "I'd like to ask you to tell me, again, about Friday."

"Friday."

"Please. It's important."

Friday had started like any weekday.

It had taken two trips up the stairs to get Galen out of bed, and by the time he'd finally come down, in stockinged feet, Kerri had finished breakfast and was anxious to go to school.

"Hurry up," Kerri ordered, carrying her dishes to the sink.

"There's plenty of time," Edana said. She put his pancakes in front of him, along with a jar of boysenberry jam, knowing how he hated syrup. Leaning over, she kissed the top of his head. "Take your time . . . eat your breakfast."

Kerri stomped out of the kitchen.

"Kerri," Edana called, following after her daughter.

Kerri was half way up the stairs and she stopped but didn't turn around. "What?"

Edana sighed; she knew the tone of voice very well. "Don't be so bossy all the time. You're not the mother in this family, I am."

"He's always making me late for things." Kerri turned then, a sullen look on her face.

"Listen, I don't know what's been up between you two for the past few days, but whatever it is, it had better stop. I've got too much on my mind to have you sniping at each other all day long." Except Galen doesn't snipe, she thought, just you.

"Then you make him hurry . . . you're the mother."

Edana watched, open-mouthed, as her daughter rushed up the stairs and disappeared around the corner. A door slammed a second later.

Despite the turmoil, everyone was in the car at eight.

At the school, Galen leaned across the front seat to give her a goodbye kiss, while Kerri bounded out of the back and took off without even a wave.

"What's wrong with your sister?" she asked, looking after Kerri.

"She's mad at me."

"For what?"

He shrugged his shoulders. "I'm gonna be late," he said.

"Okay, go on." She watched after him for a minute and then checked in her rear mirror to make sure that one of the kamikaze drivers wasn't racing up beside the car to let kids off—unsafely and illegally—in the middle of the circle.

When she looked back at the school yard, neither of her children were in sight.

Jeff laughed when she told him about the morning's scene, just one of many in recent days.

"Sounds like Kerri's a perfect candidate for retroactive birth control."

"Jeff!" She gave him a startled look and then had to laugh with him. "It's just that they've been at each other's throats all week, and it's not like them to argue this way."

"Well, they're kids, after all."

"Thank you for that insightful comment."

"You know what I mean."

"You think I'm making too much out of it?"

Jeff nodded. "Like they always say . . . 'this, too, shall pass.' "

"I suppose you're right." She sighed. "I guess I'm just feeling guilty; I haven't had much time for them lately. Maybe they're feeling neglected."

"Guilt and neglect . . . sounds like my family."

"Did your mother feel guilty about going to work and leaving you alone at home when you were a kid?"

"How would I know? She was never home long enough for me to ask her. Anyway, I was by myself a lot more than your kids . . . there are two of them . . . and look how I turned out."

"That's not very reassuring," she teased.

"From my friends I take this kind of abuse," he said and hugged her. "Don't worry, mama, they'll be all right."

But the tension that had been between them at breakfast was still apparent that afternoon. They had gone upstairs with barely a word between them, and for a while there was silence.

As she started dinner, however, she heard the sound of their voices, but they sounded calmer, she thought, like they were making up.

Then Galen, loudly, clearly, yelled, "No!"

Edana sat, tears streaming down her face, her eyes closed tight.

247

"Edana," Matt said, and his hand touched hers.

She took a deep breath and opened her eyes to look at him, and saw that he knew what she had known, and hidden from herself, from the first day.

"Galen wanted the car to hit him," she said, and bit her lips to stop them from trembling.

"I know," he said, and moved closer to her, taking her into his arms.

Then he held her, and she let go, crying until she was sure her heart would break, seeing Galen's face as he had looked a moment before he had stepped in front of the car.

She cried until there were no more tears, and her throat was raw, and then she fell asleep in his arms.

When she woke, he was still there, holding her. Gently she moved back away from him, her eyes searching his.

"The worst is over now, for both of you," he said, and she heard the husky sound of his voice, and saw that he had been crying too.

"Matt," she said, and lay her hand against his face.

"I love you," he said.

She went back into his arms.

Outside, the rain beat against the windows.

THURSDAY

Chapter Sixty-two

Kerri turned the brass key and heard the soft click as the door locked.

No one knew that she could lock her bedroom door; she had found the old key up in the attic and she had never showed it to anyone.

Mother would be upset if she knew, because of fires.

Fires could catch you in your sleep, her mother had told her. The time it took to unlock a door might make the difference between life and death.

Mother was afraid of a lot of things.

Kerri was not.

She put the key on top of the dresser and then went silently to the window to look out. The street lights had all been fixed, but their light was dim through the downpour of rain.

Somewhere lightning was flashing, and she heard the roll of thunder.

The storm was coming this way.

Kerri inched the window lock open, careful so that it would not squeak as it sometimes did, and then began to push the window up.

Immediately rain blew through the opening, wetting the front of her nightgown, and by the time she managed to get the window open far enough so that she would be able to get through, she was drenched and the floor was covered with beads of water.

But the thunder rippled and she did not care about anything but getting out.

She pushed the screen open and crawled up to kneel on the window sill before sliding a leg out. She had done this so many times before that she did not hesitate. Her foot found the tree limb and she swung her other leg through.

The tricky part was balancing on the branch and leaning out far enough so that she could clear the screen while still holding on to it, to keep it from slamming. With the wind and the slippery surface beneath her feet it was more difficult than usual, but she was determined and there was little she couldn't do if she put her mind to it.

As long as no one saw her.

She sat on the branch and looked down at the ground, then turned so she was on her stomach and began to lower herself. Her hands started to slip, so she let go, and dropped, breathless from the thrill of it, to the ground.

She stayed where she was long enough to make sure that she hadn't wakened anyone in the house. Then she ran quickly out from under the tree and into the street where she could look west and see the storm.

It was very close now, and she hugged herself.

Soon.

Wind gusted around her, pulling her sodden gown away from her skin and then snapping it back so hard that it stung.

Kerri laughed but the sound was carried away from her and she could hear nothing but the crack of the lightning, and the rumble of thunder.

The storm gathered force, and the flashes of brilliant white increased in number until there were too many to see.

She turned her face up to the sky and drew from it, her eyes unblinking, reflecting the light with a light of their own.

Kerri watched as a many-forked bolt of lightning reached down like the hand of God and struck the ground. Again and again, it arced through the sky and poured power into the earth.

A crackling sound drew her attention, and she turned to see electric wires catching fire along the street, and then the street lights went out.

A second later she was standing in total darkness.

There wasn't a single light on anywhere, for as far as she could see.

From above her came the last peal of thunder.

She laughed again, and the sound echoed down the darkened street.

She couldn't climb back up the tree in her nightgown, so she stripped it off and hid it under the bushes at the corner of the house.

In two minutes she was back in her room.

She turned on the little night light she kept by her bed and smiled with satisfaction . . .

In five minutes she was asleep.

Chapter Sixty-three

Rita was standing at Galen's bedside when the main power failed, and instinctively she moved closer to him. Now that he was off the respirator, he was in no immediate danger, but she didn't want him to be alone in the dark.

The cardiac monitor was equipped with a battery pack and the green light from the screen shone faintly on the boy's face, illuminating its fine-boned structure.

Looking at him, Rita gasped.

His eyes were open and he stared into the blackness, but he didn't move.

"Galen?" she whispered, not wanting anyone else to hear. If he was wakening, she wanted it to be a private act, without others crowding around him like a crowd at a zoo. "Galen."

His eyelids fluttered and his lips parted, and she leaned forward to listen just in case . . .

"Galen?" Reaching beneath the covers, she took hold of his hand and squeezed it, hoping the touch would reassure him. He must be frightened, she thought, after so many days of nothingness.

The back up lights came on just then and she looked up for just a second, but when she looked at him again his eyes were closed.

She let go of his hand and then noticed that the fine hairs on her arm were standing up as if from static electricity. As she reached to smooth them with her other hand, tiny sparks crackled and she felt a shock travel up the right side of her, and then she was numb.

Her heart pounded.

"Galen?"

"The power's out all over."

Rita looked up at Maggie who was standing by the windows. With only the dim emergency lights, it was difficult to see Maggie's face, but Rita thought she heard a hint of fear in her voice.

"It's the storm," Rita said.

"God, it's so . . . black out there."

"Then don't go out there."

"I won't," Maggie laughed nervously. "I wonder when they'll get the lights back on."

Rita didn't answer, but she rubbed her arm which still was numb and looked down at that angelic face.

When he lets them, she thought.

"Rita?"

Rita turned to see the nursing supervisor standing behind her.

"How is he tonight?" Willie asked.

"Quiet."

"It's odd . . . the whole hospital is quiet tonight." Willie came closer to the bed and after glancing at the monitors, she smiled. "Except . . . I've got a new admit for you."

"Well," Rita said, "I guess it's my lucky day."

The new admit turned out to be a male alcoholic with esophageal varices secondary to cirrhosis of the liver. He had been given 20 units of vasopressin in one hundred ml of glucose in E.R. by his family doctor, with satisfactory results.

Rita had to hold her breath while she was cleaning him up since both the alcohol and the blood he had vomited had soaked through his clothes. E.R. had to put him into a gown without bothering to wash him off.

She knew what their excuse would be; they were too busy saving him from bleeding to death to worry about a little thing like hygiene.

In her opinion, emergency room nurses were the prima donnas of the nursing profession. It would do them good to do a little of the scut work they so willingly passed off on others.

Then, when she had finished settling him in, she went to scrub so that she would not expose Galen to any of the man's contaminants. Alcoholics, in their debilitated, malnutritioned state, often harbored other illnesses, or sometimes even opportunistic parasites, and she couldn't take a chance on cross-infecting the boy.

It had been a close call, with the lymphadenitis.

It wouldn't happen again.

She was determined to protect him at any cost.

Chapter Sixty-four

Edana stirred restlessly, trying to go back to sleep. The clock's digital numbers mocked her: 4:07. Two and a half hours before the alarm would go off and her day would begin. A day—like so many others—which she could ill-afford to start off exhausted from a lack of sleep.

When Matt had left at one she'd come upstairs and had fallen almost immediately into a deep and dreamless sleep, but she'd woken when the thunderstorm passed overhead and since then had lain awake.

She closed her eyes and turned her back on the clock and tried not to think.

Her mind would give her no rest. Thoughts of Galen and Kerri and Peter raced through her head. A montage of images demanded her attention and wrenched feelings from her until she was certain she was drained.

But what bothered her most was a memory that floated just beyond recall, just flashes of sound and color which faded away when she tried to remember.

"It'll come to you," she promised herself, knowing that trying too hard was half the problem. She turned again and had to sit up to untangle the sheets.

Sitting there, alone in her bed, she thought of Matt and wondered how it would be with him.

And she was surprised that, knowing that she wanted him, she felt no guilt, no sense of betrayal. For the first time since Peter died, the wanting felt right.

How had that happened? Was it Matt, or was seven years finally enough to sever the bond between them?

There hadn't been anyone in all that time.

When she had first met Jeff, she'd thought it might be him, and for a few weeks, in her fantasies, he became her lover. But the fantasies were always followed by painful periods of self-loathing.

Later, when Jeff wanted to be more than a friend, she turned him down. It was a terrible time for both of them, since he was certain that he hadn't been mistaken about the signals she was sending him . . . and she knew he was right.

But they got through it.

Now she held his hand when he fell in love with other women—on the average of one a month—and they both knew that it was better this way.

And when she teased him and said: "I don't understand why these women let you treat them this way. I wouldn't have stood it for a minute."

And he said: "I wouldn't have done it to you."

Maybe they both believed it but the time had come and gone, and now they were friends.

She wanted to dance at his wedding, and for the first time, she thought that maybe he could dance at hers.

When Galen was well.

She drifted, imagining the waves washing up on the beach, the seagulls circling above, their cries plaintive in the wake of the storm.

The house was empty, the furniture gone, the windows like enormous vacant eyes staring at her as she walked through the rooms. The paint was chipping off the walls, crunching like the dried husks of dead insects under her feet.

"Galen?"

With nothing to absorb the sound, her son's name echoed, unanswered, and then faded away.

"Kerri?"

"Peter?"

Behind her she sensed a flurry of movement, and she turned, a smile forming on her face, expecting to see all of them. Peter alive, Galen well, Kerri . . .

"Kerri?"

None of them, only a few leaves blown through the open door and scattered across the floor by the spring wind.

"Where are you?"

A game of hide and seek.

Kerri and Galen liked games.

They were there, somewhere in the house . . . all she had to do was find them.

She searched through the rooms, and at each door she paused to catch her breath. as if knowing the emptiness of the room would knock all of the air out of her lungs, and she would die from not being ready for the blow when it came.

There was no sign of them, and she ran outside, her steps becoming halting as she neared the curb.

A car engine started down the street and she looked in that direction, and smiled when she saw it was Peter in the car, driving toward her with Galen and Kerri beside him on the seat.

Peter smiled back at her, and then looked down at the children, laughing as if they were sharing a secret she couldn't know.

She stepped off the curb and lifted her arm to wave, and she noticed that Peter's face was dripping blood, and that his skin was gray.

Something terrible had happened to Peter.

The car was headed straight for her, and she could see that Galen, too, had been hurt, his head battered and misshapen, and there was more blood, and then Kerri . . .

But it was Kerri driving the car, and the car never slowed.

Edana came awake with a jerk, cold and wet with perspiration. Swallowing and blinking into the darkness, she told herself that only it was a dream.

But she did not try to go back to sleep.

Chapter Sixty-five

The main power still wasn't on by five, and Rita had unplugged all non-essential equipment to reduce the drain on the generators. Pausing at the alcoholic's bedside, she resisted an impulse to disconnect him from the system.

How essential was it, she wondered, for this man to make it through the night?

At Galen's side she hesitated and then shut off the power to the skin temperature monitor.

The monitor continued to operate, the red LED indicator showing ninety-seven degrees.

It did not have a battery pack.

Galen was supplying the power to the machine.

A few days ago if she had been told that it was possible for a seven year old boy to have electric currents running through his body, she would not have believed it. Yes, she understood the electrical impulses of the brain and the electrical nature of the nervous system, but she would never have accepted what she now took as . . . natural.

But it *was* natural for him, and that was all that mattered.

When Maggie returned from the cafeteria, coffee and donut in hand, she looked at Rita and grimaced.

"You're not going to believe what I just heard."

"Calvin Hall escaped from police custody and blew up all of the Edison sub-stations in a twenty mile radius?" When Rita arrived for work, Hall was being blamed for any number of improbable events. She imagined that, given time, the evening nurses would find a way to connect him to the Lindbergh kidnapping.

"Worse. Your new patient has scabies."

"What?"

"His wife told the doctor that he had been itching like crazy, but that she thought it was just the DTs or something. The doctor took a scraping, and confirmed it was scabies."

"Why the hell wasn't it on the chart?"

"Beats me."

"Well they can just move him out of there, then, before he gives them to all of the other patients." Galen, she thought.

"No place to put him while he's in the shape he's in. They're going to order medication for everybody up here, including us, my dear."

Rita had to force herself to keep from screaming. She counted to ten, three times, and then shrugged her shoulders.

"That's the breaks," she said, and walked away.

The thought that Galen might have contracted scabies because of that wasted wreckage of a human being infuriated her. She had been careful, going back and forth between them, to wash after every contact, but had she done enough?

Were, even now, the microscopic parasites burrowing under that tender skin?

Why hadn't she listened to her instincts? She *knew* there was a reason for her intense dislike of the man.

Dislike? She hated him.

There was really only one thing she could do.

She could not undo what had already been done, but she could punish the one responsible.

One more death.

But how should she do it? With the current hysteria about the other patient deaths, how could she kill the man without being found out?

A drug overdose was the most obvious method but also the one that would be most suspect. She ruled it out reluctantly.

Then it came to her.

The medication he had been given in E.R. often induced water intoxication in patients with blood loss.

If his electrolytes were out of balance, and his fluid output continued to be impaired . . .

Water intoxication would first show up as lethargy, mental confusion, and listlessness. If untreated—if aggravated—it would result in neuromuscular hyperexcitability, stupor, convulsions, coma . . . and death.

It could be done, she thought.

A few more units of the vasopressin, eliminate the potassium being added to his IV . . .

She would do it.

She might need to volunteer for a few hours of overtime, to be absolutely sure that no one realized what was going on, but, after all, she was a dedicated nurse and no one would question her willingness to help out. Hadn't she come in on her night off?

Rita smiled and went to work.

Chapter Sixty-six

Edana lay on her side, watching as the morning lightened. Any minute now the alarm would go off and the day would start, and she would just have to get on with it, tired or not.

She could never remember ever being this tired before. Her arms and legs were heavy and tingling from lack of sleep. Even in the first days after she'd brought the twins home, coping alone with the demands of two tiny babies, she'd never felt so bone weary.

For a moment she was tempted to bury her head under the covers and forget about everything.

"Later," she promised herself, "when Galen's home." And with a groan she turned over to reach for the alarm clock before it could ring.

The clock face was blank.

"Oh no." The power was out again. She sat up quickly and grabbed her watch which showed it to be exactly six-thirty.

So she wasn't late starting a day she hardly had the

energy to face.

In the kitchen she flicked the light switch on and off, hoping that maybe the clock was just another one of the casualties of the house's rather eccentric wiring. It wasn't uncommon, with two appliances sharing the same plug, for one to work while the other didn't.

Electricians, over the years, had not been able to offer an explanation for these events, and she'd finally given up trying to figure it out.

But the kitchen light stayed off and when she tried to turn the radio on, it remained mute. She dug out a little portable and set it on the counter to play, and then went to the refrigerator to see what she could dig up for breakfast.

She was sniffing the milk to see if it had spoiled when the news came on.

"Lightning is being blamed for a power black-out in northern Orange County. Officials say that direct strikes were reported at several locations in Fullerton, Brea and Placentia, and that it may be several hours before power is restored to homes and businesses in those areas. Power was disrupted shortly after two a.m."

Edana turned, looking at the radio curiously.

"That can't be right," she said. The clock in her room had been on after four . . .

"What's that?"

John was standing in the doorway, and although he smiled at her, she thought she had never seen him look so haggard and drawn.

"Oh, nothing . . . the power's out and I was just

266

listening to them talk about it on the radio." She paused. "How do you feel this morning?"

"About half dead." He squinted at her. "You don't look so hot either."

"I couldn't sleep."

"That's all I think I *can* do. I had a notion of having some breakfast, but maybe I'll just go back to bed."

"Do you want me to bring breakfast up to you?"

"No," he said, "I think I'll try starving this cold and see if it helps."

"I think it's feed a cold."

"What do you feed a California cold?" he muttered, turning to leave. "Quiche? That runny, gooey cheese?"

Edana smiled and then looked into the open refrigerator, hoping the power would come on before all the food in the freezer turned into a runny, gooey mess.

Kerri was dressed and eating breakfast before it occurred to Edana, belatedly, that the elementary school most likely would be closed because of the power outages.

"Oh no," she said, turning from the sink and looking at her daughter. "Kerri . . . they won't be having school today."

Kerri's expression did not change. "Oh," she said.

"What am I going to do with you?"

"I can stay home . . ."

"No, your grandfather isn't feeling well, and he's trying to sleep."

"I'll be quiet."

"Even if you could be that quiet, I don't want you in the house all day with no electricity." She noticed a smile flicker across Kerri's face. "You'll just have to come with me to the hospital."

Chapter Sixty-seven

Megan noticed Edana Morgan standing in the lobby with a dark-haired little girl. Edana was talking intently to the child, who nodded and then flopped down into a chair with apparent resignation.

Curious, Megan walked up to them.

"Good morning," she said.

"Oh, Dr. Turner, good morning."

Edana's smile showed the sorrow behind it, and Megan guessed that Kennedy had told her about Galen after all. It couldn't have been easy on either of them. That Edana could smile at all suggested that she was holding up . . . and holding on.

The girl was watching them and Megan turned to her with a smile. "This must be Kerri."

"Kerri," Edana smiled, "this is Galen's doctor, Dr. Turner."

"Hello."

One word, spoken almost guardedly, and Megan instinctively sensed the child's disinterest.

"The power's off at our house," Edana was explaining, "and they're not having school, so I brought Kerri with me."

Kerri frowned and Megan noticed that the girl's jaw was tensed, as if she were angry.

Edana leaned down to kiss her daughter. "I won't be long," she promised. "I know it's boring for you to wait down here all by yourself . . ."

"She can wait up in the ICU waiting room," Megan said. "They usually don't allow children on the upper floors, but if she stays in the one room, I don't think anyone would mind. It'll be closer for you, if you have to keep running back and forth."

"Could she? That would be great."

"I think I can arrange it." She looked at Kerri. "You're too young to visit your brother, but you can at least be on the same floor."

"So, Kerri," Megan said, when Edana had gone to see Galen, "you must be lonely without your brother at home."

Icy blue eyes studied her. "Not really."

"No? I'm a little surprised to hear you say that; your mom tells me that you two are very close."

Kerri frowned. "Yes," she said, almost doubtfully. "Galen is doing well."

Again, that disinterested look.

"You don't have to stay with me," Kerri said, going to the window. "I'm just fine on my own."

Megan knew she had been dismissed.

Megan walked down the hall toward ICU, trying to sort out her reaction to Kerri Morgan.

The child was certainly different from what she had

expected.

Despite the obvious physical resemblance between mother and daughter, Megan would never have imagined them related to each other. Kerri was so withdrawn, almost isolated . . .

Perhaps, though, Kerri was merely reacting to the near-fatal injury her brother had sustained. Children's fears, Megan knew, often took unexpected forms of expression.

And there was also a possibility that Kerri could be feeling guilt over her part in the accident.

Hadn't Edana said that the children were arguing right before it all happened?

Guilt, baseless or not, was a destructive emotion.

The quote by Decimus Junius Juvenalis, memorized when she was in school, came fresh to her mind:

"This is his first punishment, that by the verdict of his own heart, no guilty man is acquitted."

A guilty child could be convicted in her own heart and mind.

Convicted and condemned.

In ICU she quickly reviewed Galen's chart.

The morning lab slips were clipped to the front and she noted that all of the boy's blood values were within normal limits. The final report on the latest EEG had been filed, and she glanced through the tracings before reading the text.

Brain wave activity was essentially normal for a person in a "sleep state."

Vital signs were also normal.

If all of the clinical findings were to be believed, the boy could be coming out of the coma.

Chapter Sixty-eight

Kerri stood at the door, looking down the empty hallway. No one had come by for several minutes, but she waited, getting a feel for it before deciding that it was safe for her to leave the waiting room.

Walking carefully so that her shoes made no sound, she went toward the stairs. The door leading into the stairwell was a heavy one, but she managed to pull it far enough so she could slip through.

The stairwell smelled of wet cement.

And, much fainter, of blood.

She knew she had to go up.

The place where she and Galen were kept as babies was on the fifth floor.

She began to climb the stairs slowly, taking care to step lightly so that her footsteps wouldn't echo and give her away. Hand on the rail, she went steadily upward.

When they were five their mother had taken them to a party given by the hospital especially for all of the babies who were born too early. Babies who, like them, had needed special care.

Kerri had been surprised at how many children were there. She and Galen had been among the oldest, and they were the only twins.

"Miracle babies," she could remember someone saying.

"Tiny miracles," said another.

Kerri had quickly tired of it. She did not like people touching her and patting her on the head. She did not like the kisses from teary-eyed nurses who pretended to know who she was; she knew they were only reading the name tag she wore.

Retreating to a corner of the room, she had come across some pictures of what they called 'the unit.' Standing there, she had felt something stirring inside of her.

"Can I see?" she asked her mother, pointing to the pictures.

"Oh, no, honey, children can't go up there."

"I want to see." She took a step closer to the pictures and touched one.

"There are a lot of sick babies there, Kerri. They need their rest and we mustn't disturb them."

Kerri frowned. "I want to see," she repeated.

Her mother swatted her lightly on the bottom. "Behave yourself . . ."

Galen had come up to them and Kerri reached and grabbed his arm, pulling him to stand beside her, and pointing at the photographs.

"Look," she said, lowering her voice.

Galen looked where she was pointing, and then back at her.

"Where we were," she said urgently.

He smiled at her and then they stood, looking, until their mother pulled them away.

Ever since then Kerri had been waiting for another chance to see.

This was it.

The floor levels were marked on the inside of the doors, and when she saw the number five, she stopped, listening for any noise that might indicate someone else was in the stairwell. All she heard was the sound of her own breathing.

There was a small window in the door, and by standing on her toes she could just manage to see through it. Satisfied that no one was nearby, she pushed the door open and let herself through.

The wall on the opposite side of the hall was entirely glass, and through the glass she could see the shapes and colors that she had memorized from the photograph.

"Where we were," she breathed.

There were blue-gowned nurses inside the glass walls, but they did not see her as she walked slowly along the hall. She wondered if any of them had been there when she and Galen were born.

The babies were inside incubators.

She knew they were incubators because her mother had told her that's what they were after she had watched a program about early babies on the news.

None of these babies looked real to her. They didn't move much, and their little faces reminded her of the monkeys she'd seen at the San Diego Zoo.

Even so, she had been like them.

Kerri pressed closer to the glass.

Kerri heard the door to the stairwell open, and she moved quickly down the hall until she was past the lighted nurseries. Standing with her back against the glass, she waited nervously for someone to approach her, but after a minute she decided that whoever it was had gone the other way.

Turning to start back, she saw that behind the glass, hidden in darkness, was a room like where the babies were. The empty incubators were almost invisible in the shadows, but she was sure that they were surrounded by the machines . . . the special machines that were the connection.

Kerri saw the way in.

No one saw her.

She moved from one machine to the next, touching every one of them, feeling the current flow from the cool metal casings into her body.

Then she found the center of the room and stood with eyes closed, waiting for the power to come to her. In the still air of the room her perspiration smelled of ozone.

Around her, one by one, colored indicator lights began to flash . . . red, blue, green, yellow . . . in rhythm with her heartbeat.

The connection was complete.

This was the source.

Chapter Sixty-nine

Rita threw the pen on the desk, leaned back in her chair and rubbed the back of her neck.

"Thank God that's over," she said.

One of the day nurses looked up and nodded wearily. "I don't know what we would have done without you."

Rita smiled. "You'd have managed."

"It's too bad . . . all that work, and we still lost him."

"Well," Rita said, getting to her feet, "what is it they say? 'To all things there is a season . . . a time to live and a time to die.' "

"I guess. Going home now?"

"I'd better if I plan on being back here at seven tonight."

"I don't know how you do it," the day nurse said, shaking her head. "Or even why you do it. I mean, working seventeen hours, running home to sleep for six and then coming back for another twelve?"

"Just dedicated," Rita said, and glanced at the sheet-covered form across the room. "Some things are more important than a little sleep."

Waiting for the elevator, Rita watched as Galen's mother started down the hall toward the waiting room.

For a while, this morning, Rita had debated whether to tell Mrs. Morgan about Galen opening his eyes. She decided against it, primarily because she suspected that his mother would increase the number and duration of her visits, hoping to be at the bedside when it happened again.

Rita knew the time was coming when he would awaken and she wanted to be the one who was with him when he did.

She couldn't share him, even with his mother.

Not when she had done so much for him.

It was her reward.

It was her right.

Chapter Seventy

When the cab pulled up in front of the police station, Calvin sprang for it like the dogs of hell were at his heels.

"Where to?"

"Anywhere," Calvin said fervently, "just get me away from here."

"I hear ya."

With excruciating slowness, the cab pulled away from the curb and merged smoothly into traffic.

Calvin had to close his eyes. "Thank God."

He hadn't really believed that they would let him go.

He had expected to see someone run out of the station after him, expected the cab door to be yanked open, expected to be dragged by the scruff of his neck back inside.

He could scarcely believe his luck.

They hadn't arrested him.

He was free.

He took his handkerchief from his pocket and wiped his steaming face.

"You okay?" the cab driver asked, looking at him

in the rear view mirror.

Calvin could only nod.

In a few minutes he was able to talk well enough to give his address.

The driver repeated it and then asked: "So . . . what happened back there?"

"What?"

"The P.D. You don't look like you were picked up for jaywalking."

"No . . ." He heard the near-sob in his own voice and covered his mouth with his hand.

The driver must have heard it too, because he shut up, then.

Calvin stared unseeing out the window.

He could feel the curious eyes watching him as he walked across the courtyard toward the apartment. Digging for his keys, he prayed that no one would try to talk to him.

No one did.

He had decided, in the long hours he'd spent waiting for one detective or the other to question him, that if it was ever over, if he was ever free of this, he would change his life completely.

He would move, get a new job, maybe color his hair, grow a mustache, learn to dance, and, most importantly, never, never, *ever* get near a hospital again.

The hospital was the cause of all of his troubles.

Being around dying people was just asking for misery, and he had already had more than his share.

When the time came, he would die in a gutter.

It was safer.

He made one last call to the police station to verify

that he was free to leave town. He wanted to make absolutely sure that he could board a plane without a hand reaching out to pull him back.

When the sun went down he left the apartment for the last time, taking only what he could carry. He'd left a note for the landlady, telling her she could do whatever she wanted with what was still in the apartment.

He omitted a suggestion about where she might want to store it all while she made up her little mind.

And although he knew she was watching him, he no longer cared. She had done her best to ruin his life, and she had failed. The police hadn't told him how they happened to get his note, but he knew.

He walked, carrying his two suitcases, to the bar where he'd left his car. Laughter floated out the open door, along with the yeasty smell of beer.

For a minute he stood, breathing it in, and then he shook his head. No, he didn't belong here any more than anywhere else he'd ever been.

The car started on the first turn of the key.

A good omen, he thought.

Chapter Seventy-one

"You're very quiet," Edana commented, glancing at Kerri. "Are you feeling all right?"

"I just want to get home and go to bed," Kerri said.

"I'm sorry we stayed so long at the hospital, but I called Grandpa earlier and he said the lights were still out at home . . . I didn't want to go home to a dark house." She stopped for a red light and looked at her daughter.

Kerri did not answer, gazing steadily out the window.

In the fading light, Edana thought Kerri looked a little pale, and her eyes were bright, as if filled with unshed tears.

"Kerri," she said, "when Galen is home again and everything is back to normal, maybe you and I can spend some time together. I know it probably seems to you that all your grandfather and I ever talk about is Galen, but that's only because he's so very sick."

"He's not sick," Kerri said. "He's hurt."

"That's true, but you know what I mean. He's in the hospital, all alone, and I want to spend as much time with him as I can."

Kerri continued to stare out the window.

"It may not even be that much longer. Can you hang in there for a while?" She started to reach across to touch Kerri's arm, but the light changed and she had to shift gears. "I'll tell you what . . . you choose what you want for dinner tonight. Anything you want, just name it."

Kerri shook her head. "I'm not hungry anymore."

The 'anymore' caught her attention. "Did you get something out of the machines at the hospital?"

Kerri's laughter was a surprise.

"I did," Kerri said, sounding very adult. "I got everything I needed out of the machines."

When they got home, as promised, Kerri went straight to her room.

The lights were on, although they kept dimming and brightening, and John was settled in front of the television with a cup of tea and a towering stack of toast.

"What's with Kerri?" he asked, after watching her march up the stairs without a word.

Edana collapsed on the couch beside him. "I don't know, but don't rent a tuxedo to wear to the Mother of the Year awards banquet; I think I've been disqualified."

"You're a good mother," he said, and patted her hand.

She tried to smile but gave it up for a sigh. "Sometimes I just don't understand her."

"Just sometimes?"

"Make that a lot of the time. I get the feeling when I'm talking to her that she doesn't even hear me. Like I don't exist in her world."

"Well," John said thoughtfully, "she's always been an independent little thing. Even when she could barely walk, she had a mind of her own."

"That doesn't bother me; I don't want her to be a little 'yes man.'"

"Ha! She's never been that."

"I just wish she'd let me closer to her."

"I'd like to be able to give you some advice, but Mary and I only raised Peter . . . I don't know much about raising little girls."

"Maybe it's my fault that she's this way."

"How's that?"

She looked at her hands folded in her lap and twisted her wedding ring around her finger. "I've thought about it, and maybe . . . because Galen was so much like Peter . . . maybe I gave him too much love, and Kerri not enough."

"Edana," John said gently, "love can't be measured out in purely equal doses. It doesn't work that way. But I do know that some people are just plain harder to love than others. They make you work at loving them . . . but it's in *them*, not in you."

"But children?"

"Children too. Those people who say that it's all upbringing that makes a child turn out one way or the other haven't got their heads on straight. Some of it is born in, and nothing you can say or do will ever change the way those kids are meant to be."

Edana frowned. "I feel bad for Kerri."

"Don't. Kerri knows that you love her, and are

ready to love her more." He paused. "I've never said anything about it, but I've watched you, over the years, try to get through to that little girl. She's my only granddaughter, and I love her dearly, but I have to say she hasn't made it easy for you. It's crossed my mind, once or twice, that it's because she's jealous that Galen loves you. I think she wants him all to herself."

"Not now," Edana murmured. "She doesn't seem to care about him at all."

"Yes, I've noticed that she's a little distant, right now, when it comes to her brother, but I think she'll get over it. Mary used to say it's a thin line between love and hate. I think the trouble with Kerri is right now that line's a little blurred."

"So what do I do?"

"I think you just have to wait it out. Concentrate on getting Galen home and healthy. The rest will fall into place; things have a way of settling themselves, if you leave 'em alone. Time works any number of miracles if you let it."

Edana leaned over and hugged him. "I could use a good miracle about now."

"Couldn't we all?"

After John had gone to bed, Edana went around the house locking up and turning off lights.

As she started to pull the shades down in the living room, she saw something white under the bushes at the corner of the house. She watched for a moment, thinking it was the white cat from across the street, but when she tapped on the window it didn't move.

She turned the porch light back on and went outside. The ground was soggy from all the rain and it pulled at her shoes as she got closer to the bushes.

From here it looked like a towel or something, perhaps blown off a clothesline in last night's storm.

But when she pulled a corner of it, she saw that it was a nightgown. A white flannel nightgown like Kerri wore.

"What is this doing out here?"

She held it up and away from her and then looked up at Kerri's bedroom window.

After wringing it out, she tossed the nightgown in the washing machine, but decided against starting a load of laundry. She was just too tired.

At Kerri's door she paused and listened. All was quiet.

Tomorrow was soon enough to ask Kerri why her nightgown had been hidden under the bushes. Kerri had been upset enough about spending the day at the hospital; there was no sense in making matters worse.

But once in bed, she wondered if it was diplomacy that kept her from knocking on Kerri's door. Wasn't she relieved that her daughter was apparently asleep?

The truth was, she had not wanted to confront Kerri.

Was she afraid of her own child?

What about the dream?

Chapter Seventy-two

Matt saw the last of the lights go off in Edana's house.

He had been parked down the street from the house since just after he got off work, trying to build up the nerve to go up to the door. He hadn't, but neither had he been able to make himself drive away.

Last night, when he told her he loved her, she had come into his arms like she'd always belonged there, but as he held her, kissing her, she had said her late husband's name.

Peter.

It was almost like a cry, and he didn't even think that she knew what she was saying, but the word chilled his heart.

Peter.

Today he had struggled with himself, uncertain whether to call her, but knowing what she would think if he didn't. He could easily say that he had been tied up in court, or on an investigation, and he knew that she would believe whatever he said.

More than once he'd dialed the hospital's number, but he hung up each time before it began to ring.

He had never lived through a day that passed so slowly.

Sitting in the car, he had watched as she drove up with Kerri. The temptation was strong to walk up to her and pretend nothing was wrong.

Was there anything wrong?

It was crazy to be jealous of a dead man.

But there it was, and he couldn't deny it, at least not to himself. He had to be more to her than a stand-in.

Now the lights were out, and he had to get through the night without seeing her or talking to her. And by tomorrow he would have to decide what the hell to do.

All he really wanted to do was love her.

Chapter Seventy-three

Galen could hear voices.

Hushed, speaking softly, the voices floated in his head, and he tried to make out what they were saying, but the words . . . if they were words . . . made no sense.

He was coming out of the blackness, and it hurt.

His head hurt more than anything else.

It had hurt since even before the sound. The sound had ripped at him, tearing into him, but the pain had been first.

He flexed his hands, moving his fingers and stretching them, feeling a tightness in the movement, but it was not an unpleasant sensation.

Still, he was unable to do it for very long.

His hand curled around the power cords and he felt the power pulsing in his grip, but it was not enough, yet, to make the pain go away.

Soon, he thought.

"Galen."

Someone was standing near him.

"Galen, can you hear me?"

He tried to open his eyes.

"I won't let them hurt you, Galen."

A hand, cool and gentle, caressed his face.

"No one will ever hurt you again."

The darkness lightened but all was clouded and he could not see.

"I'll take care of you and you won't ever have to worry again."

FRIDAY

Chapter Seventy-four

Rita had noticed before that the night nursing supervisor was particularly interested in Galen's care. Every time that Willie Thompson came in, she always made a point of reading the boy's chart meticulously.

And Willie always, always, went over to the bedside to touch him.

At first that had bothered Rita in a way, but she'd quickly realized that it was good strategy to have an ally. As much as she would like, there was no way that she could work every night, and Willie might be able, when Rita wasn't there, to keep an eye on Galen.

She wondered if she could confide in Willie.

Was it safe?

Rita watched Willie as the other woman talked on the phone. A nice face, she thought, not pinched and hard like some of the other supervisors. A mouth always ready to smile, and warm brown eyes.

She knew that Willie had a reputation as an excellent nurse and even more as a fair and even-handed supervisor. She *listened* to the nurses when they had a complaint, or a suggestion, or even a fear.

That's what the talk was, anyway.

In the dealings that Rita had had with her in the past, she had been impressed at Willie's willingness to reserve judgment until all sides of an issue had been examined.

It was important, if she was going to tell someone about Galen, that they hear her out and keep an open mind.

Rita knew some people might think she was crazy for believing what she did, but she had proof she was right.

Last Friday when he'd been admitted, when he was wired into the life support systems, all the lights flashing brightly, like it was Christmas.

The way he always twisted his arm through the power lines.

And she could still feel the vague numbness in her right side from where he'd sent his message through her.

She knew he needed her to help him with his mission. Even with the powers he possessed, he had been badly injured and wasn't able to do it on his own.

Galen was, she felt inside of her, the second son of God. It would be many years before he was ready to go among the people, and he had to be protected until that time came.

She would be his protector.

No one would harm him as long as she was around.

And when she wasn't around . . . Rita looked at Willie speculatively.

She had not grown up believing in God, although she'd been baptized a Methodist as a child.

It had meant nothing to her then . . . a paper-thin

wafer which melted on her tongue, and grape juice which was supposed to be the blood of Christ. To her, the church was just a building where, during the week, she could run and play with the minister's daughter.

Going to church was just something people did.

When the family moved away the year she was ten, she hadn't even given a thought to leaving the church behind. Somehow, her parents had never gotten around to joining another. She hadn't minded.

At first, when she realized that Galen was not an ordinary child, she wondered why she had been chosen to care for His son. But then she understood.

It was because He wanted a non-believer.

If she had been like one of the impassioned followers, she would have been plagued with doubts as to her own worthiness for the task. In the presence of a Supreme Being, a believer would be held immobile by awe and reverence.

Rita, although she loved His son dearly, was less wonder-struck.

She knew it was her duty to protect him, and she would.

As soon as she thought he was able, she would take him away from here, take him somewhere he would be safe.

Away from the other one.

When Willie went to get a cup of coffee in the back, Rita decided to act.

She got to her feet a little unsteadily, feeling her head swim as her body protested the too-few hours of sleep she'd gotten. Instead of sleeping for the six hours between her shifts, she had only slept two, using the other time to make calls, arranging for the cabin, arranging for a rental car.

She wanted to be ready when the time came, and she sensed that it was coming soon.

But just in case it happened when she wasn't by his side, she needed Willie.

"Willie?"

The supervisor looked up at her and smiled. "How are you holding up?"

Rita knew she was talking about work. "I'm a little tired, but I'll get through."

"I don't know how you do it. Do you want some coffee? You look like you could use some."

Rita detected concern in the way that Willie was looking at her. "Okay, sure," she agreed.

Willie poured coffee into a styrofoam cup and handed it to her.

"Willie," Rita said, taking the cup, "can I talk to you?"

"Sure. Something wrong?"

Rita glanced over at the open door and then reached to swing it shut. "It's about Galen."

Chapter Seventy-five

"Not the Second Coming of Christ, but God's second son," Rita whispered and then smiled. "And He has come to help us, and I am here to serve Him."

Willie was silent.

"He has the source of all power in Him, but He is still too young to do His Father's work. He must be nurtured, and I have been chosen to care for Him. I have to take Him from here, to where He'll be safe."

"Safe?"

"The Other is nearby."

Willie nodded as if she understood.

"I felt his power tingling up my arm," Rita said, "and it flashed like a Fourth of July sparkler out of my fingertips." Rita peered at her intently. "I can still feel it, a little." She held her arm out and spread her fingers wide as if admiring her own hand as an instrument of God.

Willie was profoundly disturbed.

Last year she had taken a continuing nursing education class which had, among other things, examined the effects of too little sleep on the human mind and body.

In addition to the expected problems of fatigue, increased irritability and depression, there had been instances where depriving a person of sleep was enough to trigger psychotic behavior.

Rita, Willie suspected, was suffering from delusions.

Willie's first impulse, listening as Rita talked, was that she should relieve her immediately of Galen's care. But she knew that Rita would never agree, and Willie was afraid of what the woman might do if anyone tried to make her leave his side.

Would she, in the guise of protecting Galen, somehow harm him?

Willie couldn't take that chance.

"I know I can trust you," Rita was saying, "I've seen you with him."

It occurred to her, with all the talk of spiriting the boy out of the hospital, that it was safer if she kept Rita's trust. At least if Willie knew what Rita was planning, she had a chance to stop her.

"I see," she said seriously, and nodded.

"Am I right?" Rita asked, a little breathlessly.

"You may be right."

Rita's eyes glinted. "I knew you'd understand."

"I do understand, Rita." Rita was watching her expectantly, obviously waiting for something else, and Willie took a sip of coffee, delaying, for a moment, the need to say more. She wasn't sure what she *could* say without setting Rita off. And even though she knew what the answer would be, she asked: "Have you told anyone else about this?"

"No . . . there's no one else. It's just between us."

Willie walked down the darkened hall, resisting the temptation to look back and see if Rita was watching her.

When she was certain that she was out of sight of ICU, she went to a wall phone and signalled the operator.

It was the middle of the night, but something had to be done, and she didn't think it could wait for morning.

As much as she wanted to believe it, she couldn't convince herself that Rita's mental state was a temporary condition. Lack of sleep may have contributed to the exacerbation of the symptoms, but the underlying psychosis had to have been there before to result in delusions such as these.

God's second son.

They didn't dare use security guards. Rita would know the minute she saw the uniforms that Willie had betrayed her.

After a quick call to the staff psychiatrist, Willie spoke to the emergency room doctor who agreed with the psychiatrist's recommendation that Rita should be sedated.

Willie enlisted two orderlies, and along with the E.R. doctor, they pretended to be bringing up a new admit.

Rita glanced at them but did not appear to be alarmed.

It was over in a matter of seconds. Whatever the doctor used to sedate her worked quickly, and they took Rita away.

Willie looked at the boy's face.

He was resting quietly.

At least, Willie thought, he's safe.

Chapter Seventy-six

The highway was dark and there were few other cars driving at this time of night.

Edana resisted the impulse to drive faster, even though at this rate it would be after one before they got home. She wasn't familiar with the road, and she didn't want to come upon a sudden curve at too high a rate of speed.

The twins slept soundly in the back seat, tired from their day at the zoo.

It had been a beautiful day. The sky was clear and the air was just warm enough to go without sweaters.

There was something special about being outdoors on a nice day. They had walked through the zoo grounds, taking their time, reading all the information placards about the animals. Galen liked the lions and tigers best, but Kerri seemed more interested in a young pair of bear cubs.

"Twins, like us," she said.

They ate too much junk food and loved every minute of it.

"Why can't we have hot dogs like this at home?" Galen asked.

"We do have hot dogs, sometimes."

"Not like these."

And she had to agree. Maybe it was the fresh air, or the sun at their backs, or just the novelty of eating as they walked along, but Edana couldn't remember ever tasting anything better.

When she absolutely couldn't take another step—the twins were still going strong—she collapsed on a bench, kicking off her shoes and watching as they ran back and forth between the exhibits.

The day passed serenely.

They stayed until closing time and then Edana took them down near the beach to a seafood restaurant she had once gone to with their father.

"What did Daddy have?" Galen asked.

"Galen, that was at least nine years ago," Edana said.

"Don't you remember?"

She had to laugh at the affronted look on her son's face, but in fact she did remember, as she remembered all of their special evenings. "He had an enormous lobster."

"That's what I want."

Although she knew he wouldn't be able to eat much, after all the snacks at the zoo, she let him order a lobster.

The waiter raised his eyebrows but did not comment.

When they left the restaurant it was late, and it was cold outside. The wind was off the ocean, and they hurried to the car and its relative warmth.

302

"Time to go home," she said.

By the time she had reached the highway, they were already asleep in the back.

The steering wheel tugged sharply to the right and she gripped it hard, cursing under her breath.

A flat tire.

She pulled off into the emergency lane and turned on her hazard lights, then sat fuming at her own stupidity in not having bought new tires as she had planned to. She had put it off one weekend too long.

Across the highway, behind a chain link fence, she could see the small twin domes of the nuclear power plant . . . San Onofre. Were there guards on at night? Probably so. In fact she saw someone moving outside, walking along a row of parked cars that she imagined belonged to the employees. She couldn't see clearly, but she thought he was in a uniform of some sort.

The center divider, however, looked impenetrable.

It was a very dark stretch of road.

This was the middle of the night.

She had two children sleeping in the back seat.

No. She was not going to try to get over there, deserted highway or not.

She would wait for a highway patrolman. That was what the auto club said to do.

"Mommy," a voice said from the back, "are we home?"

"No, honey." If she told Galen about the flat tire he would insist on helping her try to change it. She did not want her son standing by the car if a drunk came by and plowed into them. *She* did not want to be there either, drunk or no drunk. "I'm just going to rest my eyes for a while, and then we'll go on. Go back to sleep."

Then she waited.

An occasional car went by but none of them stopped.

None were police cars.

She shifted in the front seat, sitting so her back was against the passenger door, facing the power plant.

The lights taunted her.

Inside, she thought, was a phone.

Maybe if she ran out to the center divider, she could yell loud enough for one of the guards to hear her. As still as the night was, her voice should carry that far.

Just a short run. She wouldn't go until she was positive there were no cars coming. Five minutes, maybe, out of the car, and she'd be right back. And then help would come and they'd be on their way home.

Unless . . .

She waited a while longer.

She held her wrist in front of the dash, trying to see, as the turn indicators blinked, what time it was.

Three-twenty.

"Oh God," she said softly.

Again she looked over at San Onofre.

She didn't want to wait any longer.

She stood looking down the highway and tried not to think about tripping and falling, or twisting her ankle, or a car being driven with no lights.

There really was no other choice, unless she wanted

304

to wait for daybreak.

And she didn't.

After a few tentative steps, she ran quickly, and was at the divider before she knew it.

From here she could see the domes clearly. Everything looked very still. She did not see anyone outside.

"Damn," she said, and turned back to look at the car . . .

A siren went off . . .

Kerri was looking out the window at her . . .

Kerri's eyes were . . .

Edana awoke, bolting upright, and felt her pulse racing.

"Oh no," she whispered, "oh no."

It wasn't a dream.

It had happened.

Chapter Seventy-seven

Matt pushed the doorbell a second time and then glanced at his watch, wondering if he had come too early. Then he wondered if she had seen him and decided against opening the door.

But the door did open, and Edana was standing in front of him.

"Matt . . ." she seemed a little perplexed.

"I know, it's early, but I need to talk to you."

"Come in, then." She pushed the screen door open. "I was fixing breakfast . . . talk to me in the kitchen."

Morning sunlight streamed through a window over the kitchen sink, and looking at Edana, he tried to think how to begin.

She smiled at him, but waited for him to speak first.

"The other night . . . when we talked, I told you that I love you."

"I remember."

"I didn't ask you how you feel about me, because I know how things have been for you with Galen's accident. I didn't want to pressure you at all, and I still don't . . . but I need to know if you think you could be happy with me."

"Matt . . ."

"I know . . . we hardly know each other. Maybe it's unfair for me to even ask. But I knew the first time I saw you that I could love you. What I'm asking, really, is can you love me?"

She looked at him for what seemed to him to be an eternity before answering.

"Yes, I think I can."

He wanted to go to her and take her in his arms, but first he had to settle the rest of it, even if it meant that he would never hold her again.

"The other night," he said evenly, "after I kissed you, you called me by your husband's name."

She blinked. "Oh, Matt, I'm so sorry."

"I want to know . . . I want you to tell me . . . was it really me you were responding to, or . . ."

Edana crossed the room and stood before him, looking up at him, and then she reached to gently, lovingly touch his face. "It was you," she whispered. "It *is* you." And she kissed him.

He could breathe again.

Chapter Seventy-eight

Kerri slowed as she approached the school.

Scott was standing with a group of other boys, and she could tell they were watching her. Waiting for her to pass by them.

There was no way to avoid them, Kerri knew, and she lowered her eyes, determined not to look at them, no matter what they said.

"Kerri," one them called, "oh Kerriiii."

"How's Galen?" That was Scott; she knew his voice.

She did not answer, walking quickly past them.

They fell in behind her, laughing and jostling each other, and saying things that she couldn't quite hear, but which she knew she wouldn't like.

"My mom called the hospital, and they said he was doing better . . ." Scott again.

Kerri felt the heat rise in her face. She didn't want Scott to know anything about Galen, not when it was partly his fault that . . .

"My mom says when Galen gets out of the hospital, he can come over to our house for the weekend sometime."

Kerri closed her eyes and clenched her teeth.

"I've got bunk beds, and he can stay in my room."

The other boys were coming up beside her, leaning over so they could see her face, but Scott was right behind her, so close that she could feel his warm breath on her neck.

"Go away," she said.

"I won't go away," Scott taunted. "Galen's sure not anything like you . . ."

Scott had transferred into their class after Christmas vacation and Kerri had hated him from the first day.

His voice whispered in her ear. "You don't look like twins . . ."

"Go away!"

They all laughed and one of Scott's friends made a grab for her lunch, but she swung it out of his reach.

"Who will you play with, Kerri, when Galen comes to stay with me?"

Kerri whirled to face her tormentor. "He won't stay with you . . . ever."

"My mom said he . . ."

"He won't ever stay at your house." She narrowed her eyes. "And you had better stop bothering me."

"Or what? What'll you do, Kerri?" He smiled, his face three inches from hers. "Galen told me that you liked to always have your way."

"He never said that, you liar."

"He told me lots of things about you."

Kerri brought her hand up quick and slapped his face.

Scott stepped back. "You can't do anything here, can you? Not here . . . Galen told me."

Kerri ran away.

"Oh Kerri."

Kerri turned to see Mrs. Brown approaching.

"Kerri, I have some things of Galen's that maybe you'd better take home." She held up a brown paper bag. "I don't want them getting misplaced, and I'm sure he'll need them when he comes back to school."

Kerri frowned. "He's not coming back," she said.

Chapter Seventy-nine

Megan caught up to Willie Thompson just as the supervisor was about to leave the hospital.

"I know you're off duty, but I'd like to talk to you about what happened last night."

Willie looked tired but she nodded. "All right, but do you mind if it's somewhere I can sit down? All of a sudden I'm dead on my feet."

"I heard," Megan said, "that Rita is under heavy sedation on the locked ward, and they're worried she might try to kill herself."

Willie nodded. "I'm sure she feels she failed."

"Failed at what?"

"Protecting Galen Morgan."

Megan hesitated. "You're the only one who knows, firsthand, what she was trying to do."

"She told me," Willie said slowly, "but I'm not sure how much was real and how much was in her head."

"Why don't you tell me what she said?"

"It's pretty fantastic."

"There are already some fantastic rumors going around."

"Yes," Willie said with a trace of bitterness, "I'm

sure there are."

". . . I would rather know the truth."

Willie was silent for a moment, and then she began to talk.

When Willie finished she leaned back in her chair and stared up at the ceiling. "It's just so sad."

"Sad?"

"Rita was one of the best nurses we had in ICU. A little weird sometimes, but then, aren't we all weird about something or another? Yet . . . or maybe because of that . . . she was an extremely competent, very knowledgeable, dedicated and devoted nurse."

"I always thought so," Megan agreed.

"I've seen her pull patients back from death's door, patients whose doctors were ready to give up on." Willie ran a hand through her hair. "I would want her to be my nurse if I were the patient. But the same quality, the same obsessiveness, that made her an excellent nurse, also made her vulnerable."

"We're all vulnerable."

"We are, but people like Rita are more so. All she really wanted was to take care of that little boy. She just got a little crazy about it."

"I wonder."

Now Willie looked at her curiously.

Megan frowned. "I've been thinking about something Dave Levine told me. About Dr. Abrahms."

"Yes?"

"He told me that there were two holes in Abrahms' head."

"So the story goes."

312

"Tell me, Willie, if you were hurt, very badly, and someone came and hurt you more, what would you want to do?"

"Want to do? Or do?"

"Want to do."

"I'd probably want to hurt them back."

"And what if, somehow, you had the ability . . . the power, if you will, to hurt them without ever going near them?"

"I'm not following you."

"When Galen was admitted to the hospital, he was hurting. Dr. Abrahms saw him in the emergency room, and to relieve the pressure on Galen's brain, he drilled burr holes in the boy's skull."

"Which probably saved Galen's life."

"Most likely it did. But Galen wouldn't know that, when Abrahms was hurting him."

"But Galen was unconscious. Non-responsive. I read the reports myself."

"Right. And we assume if a person is unconscious, that they don't feel any pain."

"I've never thought about it that way, but I suppose you're right."

"And we don't give a head trauma patient anything that might impair their neurological responses. No analgesics."

"Right."

"So do they feel pain at a subconscious level?"

Willie looked thoughtful. "I'm sure they do, but they never seem to remember it when they wake up."

"No, but they do *feel it*. And if someone was hurting you, and your subconscious was able to hurt them back."

313

"You think Galen killed Dr. Abrahms? But, how is that possible?"

"I don't know. But I think it's more than a coincidence that Abrahms' injury was identical to the 'injury' he inflicted on Galen earlier that same night."

Willie stared at her.

"Rita told you that Galen had the source of power within him . . . what do you think she meant by that?"

"I don't know . . . she also said he was the second son of God. She said a lot of crazy things. Sparks flying . . ."

"But she said some rational things, too. She was protecting him, she said, from people who would hurt him."

Willie gasped. "Do you think Rita did it? Do you think Rita killed Abrahms?"

"I wish I knew. But somehow it's connected to Galen."

"Oh my . . ."

The sound of Megan's pager interrupted them.

"I'd better get that." She went to the phone on the wall. "Dr. Turner." Then she listened as the operator rang through to ICU. "This is Dr. Turner," she said when the ICU secretary answered. In a minute she turned to look at Willie. "All right," she said, "I'll be right there."

"What?"

"Galen's awake."

Chapter Eighty

"Call his mother," Megan said to the secretary as she passed on the way to Galen's bedside.

"I already did."

"And Dr. Stafford."

"Ditto."

Megan nodded and kept on walking.

Galen was lying, his head turned to one side, eyes open and aware. His arms, which had been almost rigid at his sides for the past week, were folded across his stomach.

"Hello, Galen. I'm Dr. Turner."

A flicker of a smile crossed his face.

"Hello."

His voice was raspy, probably because of the trach, but it sounded good to her.

"I was beginning to think that you'd never wake up," she said gently, and took his hand.

"Where's Rita?"

Megan concealed her surprise; how had he known the nurse's name? "Rita wasn't feeling too well."

"She's gone?"

"Hmm. But how about you, how are you feeling?"

"My head hurts."

"I can imagine it does." She paused. "Your mother is on her way . . . she'll be here any minute."

He closed his eyes and grimaced. "Kerri," he said.

"What?"

"Tell Kerri . . ."

Megan leaned closer.

The words came out slowly, sounding raw. "Tell her . . . to stop."

Chapter Eighty-one

Megan Turner was waiting for them at the ICU door.

"I know you're anxious to see him, but I'd like to ask you to just stay a few minutes . . . and then I'd like to talk to you."

"Is something wrong?" Edana had a sudden image of her son paralyzed or . . ."

"No," Megan said quickly, "the neurological exam hasn't been completed yet, but he seems to be fine."

Edana looked at Matt and then back at the doctor. "Whatever you think is best."

Galen was looking in her direction when she went through the door, and her heart leapt.

Seeing those blue eyes watching her, she felt dangerously close to tears, but she didn't want him to see her crying. She did not want to cry at all.

"Baby," she said, smiling down at him.

"Mom . . ."

Her mouth was trembling and the sound of his voice was almost enough to put her over the edge.

"Oh Galen." She kissed him and felt a tear fall from her lashes.

"Tell Kerri . . ." he said, ". . . to stop."

A sliver of fear, ice cold, stabbed through her heart. "What?"

But he didn't answer, putting his hand to his throat and shaking his head, his eyes strangely haunted.

Matt was standing with Megan when she came out a few minutes later.

"How is he?" Matt asked.

She could only smile, not trusting herself to talk about the sight of her son. Then she looked at Megan. "You wanted to talk to me . . . I think it's time."

Edana listened and was frightened.

"He wasn't able to talk much," Megan said, "but what he did say has me worried."

Matt looked doubtful. "Are you sure he wasn't just . . . hallucinating?"

"That occurred to me." Megan looked thoughtful. "But putting together what Galen told me and Rita told Willie Thompson, I have to believe that something . . ." she hesitated, as if searching for the right word, and then shook her head. "*Something* has happened, *is* happening . . ."

Edana closed her eyes. She knew it was true. All of the unexplainable incidents, the strange occurrences, the nightmares, the fears . . . it was true.

When she opened her eyes, Matt was looking at Megan skeptically. "If you're right . . ."

"She's right," Edana said quietly. When he turned

to her, their eyes held for a long moment and then he nodded.

"Then what do we do?" he asked. "More important, what *can* we do?"

"Where's Kerri?" Megan asked.

"Her grandfather went to pick her up from school . . . he's bringing her here . . ."

Chapter Eighty-two

"Here we are," John Morgan said, turning into the hospital parking lot and looking up at the building.

Kerri, beside him, said nothing.

She had not spoken, in fact, since her teacher brought her out of the classroom.

He frowned. What was on the child's mind, he wondered. It seemed to him that she should be a little happier to hear that her brother was out of the coma.

He was, he admitted to himself, a little annoyed at her behavior.

"Kerri?"

She still did not say anything, but she turned to look at him, her mouth set in a tight angry line.

What did she have to be mad at?

He opened his mouth to ask her just that, and reconsidered. There was a time and a place for everything, and right here and now he didn't think he was up to dealing with a petulant child.

"Come on," he said instead.

At the information desk he explained that he had a doctor's permission to take Kerri up to the ICU floor.

"No," the woman said, shaking her head, "children aren't allowed."

"I know that's true most of the time, but you see her brother is a patient there, and he just came out of a coma, and the doctor said Kerri could come to see him."

"I'll have to call." She reached for the phone.

"You do that," he said, and grabbing Kerri by the hand, he walked away.

"Wait!" he heard the woman call from behind him.

He was tired of waiting.

On the elevator he glanced down at Kerri.

"Don't worry," he said, "I'll get you in to see Galen."

A hint of a smile played at her mouth. "I'm not worried," she said.

Something about the tone of her voice bothered him; she sounded, he thought, like she was beyond anger, like she was in a cold rage.

Then the elevator doors opened and there were other things to think about.

Standing at the doors which led into ICU, John looked around the hall.

"I wonder where your mother is?" He could see through the window in the door that she wasn't in with Galen.

Galen, he could also see, was awake.

"Wait right here, Kerri, I'm going to ask the nurse." He pushed through the door.

As he approached the desk area, one of them, looking in his direction, stood up suddenly.

"She can't come in here." The nurse said, and he turned to see that Kerri had come through the door. She was standing, very still, her eyes fixed on Galen.

"Kerri . . ." he started to say.

It happened so fast that there was no time to react . . .

Kerri, her eyes glowing, her face dark with fury, whirled at them and . . .

Around him, bright lights flashed and windows shattered, blowing out in an explosive force, and a brutal wind stung his face and roared in his ears, and . . .

Above the wind he heard the screeching sound of metal tearing and rending as every piece of equipment in the room . . . everything except what was near Galen's bed . . . was forced through the gaping holes, and . . .

Not believing, he saw the others being swept out, blown clear of the building, to fall to their deaths . . .

Until all that remained was the three of them.

The room was bathed in an eerie white light.

Kerri looked at him and her eyes glittered like an animal's caught in the glare of headlights on a dark country road.

"Go away," she said.

"Go," Galen said.

He obeyed.

Chapter Eighty-three

"There isn't time to worry about how she did it," Matt said, after John finished telling them what had happened in ICU. The intercom blared pleas for doctors to report to the emergency room, and Matt had to raise his voice to be heard. "What are we going to do?"

"Let me go in there," Edana said, "they're my children."

"No."

"They . . . Kerri wouldn't hurt me."

"You don't know that."

"She let me go," John said.

"Maybe she wanted you to tell us . . . a witness . . ."

Megan interrupted. "I'm about your size," she said to Edana, "Kerri might think I was you."

Matt held up his hands. "You're all crazy."

"What do you suggest? A SWAT team?" John's face, which had been pale when he'd first come out, was now red with outrage. "Those are children in there!"

"At least one of those children are responsible for a

323

lot of people dying."

No one spoke for a moment.

"Please," Edana took Matt's hands in hers. "No police. Let me . . ."

The intercom fell suddenly silent, and around them the lights dimmed and went out.

"What," Matt asked in the hush that followed, "can you do?"

"What can the police do?" she countered.

"Edana . . ."

"They're my children . . . and I'm going in there."

"I can't let you do that," Matt said.

Chapter Eighty-four

"Kerri . . . stop."

"Why couldn't you have died?"

Galen looked at his sister and was surprised to see tears running down her face. He had never seen her cry before.

"You don't mean that."

"I do. I wanted you to die."

His throat hurt badly and there was a taste like copper in his mouth, but he had to talk anyway.

"Why?"

"You broke your promise."

"I didn't." He shook his head, and swallowed, wincing at the effort.

"It was supposed to be just us, just the two of us, forever and ever . . ."

He opened his mouth to answer, but his voice was completely gone and he felt a sharp pain as he tried to force the words out. Putting his hand to his bandaged throat, he felt a warm wetness, and when he took his fingers away there was blood on them.

Kerri, he thought, help me.

Her answer, clear and cold, echoed in his mind.

No.

Chapter Eighty-five

Edana looked at him a long time before answering. "You can't stop me," she said.

"I think she should go in," Megan agreed, "and I think I should go in with her."

Matt shook his head, his eyes holding on Edana. "We're all going to wait for the police back-up unit to arrive."

Megan stepped between Edana and Matt. "If you try to use force on her, after what she's done today, it could result in a blood bath. Let her mother and I try."

"That's all I'm asking," Edana said. "Let me try. If I can't get through to her . . ." She closed her eyes and her face contorted in pain. "If I can't get through to her, then I'll do whatever you say. But I have to try."

Chapter Eighty-six

Kerri turned to look at them as they came through the door.

"Go away." Her voice sounded odd, as if it originated in a hollow place.

A rush of wind quickened the air and Edana knew it was a warning, but she shook her head. "I'm not going, Kerri. I want to talk to you."

"Kerri," Megan said, "we want to help you."

Kerri laughed.

"Honey . . . I want to understand. About you, and Galen." As she turned her eyes toward her son, she stiffened.

There was blood dripping from the saturated bandage over the wound in his throat.

"I see it," Megan whispered.

"Kerri," Edana said urgently, "let the doctor look at Galen."

"He has to die," Kerri said.

"Why, Kerri?" Edana's heart was pounding so hard that she wasn't sure she would be able to hear the answer. No, her mind protested, no!

"Then there'll be only one of us." Kerri smiled,

and held her hands out in front of her. Her skin was aglow with white light. She turned her gaze on Megan. "Tell *her* to leave . . . and you can stay."

Edana looked fearfully at Megan. "Will he bleed to death?"

Megan shook her head. "I don't know."

Still, Edana knew, there was no choice; they had to do what Kerri wanted.

After Megan left, Edana took a step closer toward her children. Galen was watching her, his face pale and drawn.

"Kerri . . . I want to understand what has happened. Why . . . are you doing these things?"

Then, with a pain so sharp that she thought something had struck her between the eyes, she suddenly could see.

Kerri's memories . . . in her mind.

Tiny, helpless, and in so much pain.

Sharp biting pain where cold needles pierced her skin, a pressure from the other probes.

The steady pulse of machinery around her, taking the place of the heartbeat from before . . .

Hands touched her, but not with tenderness.

Always pain.

The other was gone.

There only was pain.

She had been torn from the dark, quiet, wet safety. Torn from the other.

She was alone.

She came to understand that the other was nearby. She could feel another heartbeat, and she could sense pain like her own.

Their hearts kept time.

Sometimes the hands propped her so she was facing the one who had been with her, and then she could see him.

Around them both, the machines hummed on, and through her skin she began to feel another pulse, another heartbeat, through metal veins very unlike her own.

Because there was nothing else, no other warmth, she accepted the new heartbeat as a part of her.

When she was taken away from the source, she was fretful, until there was a new place. The source was weaker, but present, and it pulsed in reassurance beyond her sight.

The other was now with her, and they became as one, breathing with the same rhythm, their hearts joined.

But as they grew, minds filled with the wonder of new tastes and sights and sounds, their awareness of the source faded.

For a while.

The other was Galen.

When they were older, Galen rediscovered the source, and he told her, and they used it.

At first it was just for fun. Games.

But she, in her dreams at night, still felt the stinging pains, still could be, in her dreams, the tiny baby that they'd hurt.

She wanted to hurt them.

Galen held her back.

329

Then Galen found a friend, and he wanted to be away from her. He did not understand that they were bound together and could not be apart. Without him, she would die.

When he realized that she wanted to hurt his friend, he was angry, and they argued.

He didn't hate like she did.

He said he would stop her . . .

He thought she couldn't do it without him . . .

Galen stepped in front of the car so that she would be without him, so that she would be alone, and to break the bond between them and the source.

But he was wrong.

She could do it all without him . . . and she had, but she was angry that he had betrayed her, angry that he had told his friend the only secret . . . the reason why they could never use the power on each other . . .

If someone knew, they were immune.

Galen had betrayed her the second time when he didn't die. She had killed the doctor so that her brother would die, but it was too late by then.

Now she would just wait, and let him die.

There would only be one again.

Released from the grip of Kerri's memories, Edana slumped to the floor, where she kneeled, waiting for her strength to return.

But *I* know now, she thought. I can save him.

"Kerri, I won't let you," she said. "I'll tell the others, and when they know, you won't be able to hurt them either."

Her daughter looked at her with pained eyes. "You can't tell everyone."

"Please Kerri, don't do this. I love you . . . I love Galen."

"There can only be one."

"Oh, God, Kerri . . ."

"He broke his promise to me."

Edana got slowly to her feet. "I'm going out there, and I'm going to tell those people, and the doctor's going to come in here and help your brother."

In her mind, Edana heard her son's voice.

The game's over.

Kerri did nothing as Edana started toward the door.

As soon as the door closed behind her, a blinding white light streamed through the small window, lighting the faces of everyone standing in the hall.

Edana whirled and put her hands up to shield her eyes, and felt a hand grab her arm.

"Back from there," yelled Matt.

"No! No!" She struggled to see, but Matt was pulling her back. "She can't hurt anyone who knows about her," she said desperately, and pulled away. "God damn it, Matt, let go!"

But he held her and she could only watch through the small frame of glass, dark shapes illuminated by light. Then, in a dizzying whirl of motion, Edana was looking out through Galen's eyes.

Kerri approached her brother.

"Galen," she said, "just one."

He reached his hand out to her. His hand, like

hers, was translucent with light, and he could see the bones beneath his skin.

"We are one," he said, and grasped her hand with his.

"Always," she said.

There was no pain as her flesh melded into his, hand to hand, their heads coming close together, and he kissed her tenderly. A heat spread through him, and then Kerri was light, seeping through his pores, and they were one.

Within him, two hearts beat as one.

Epilogue

On a clear morning in May, Edana Morgan took her son—her children—home.

THESE ZEBRA MYSTERIES
ARE SURE TO KEEP
YOU GUESSING

By Sax Rohmer

THE DRUMS OF FU MANCHU	(1617, $3.50)
THE TRAIL OF FU MANCHU	(1619, $3.50)
THE INSIDIOUS DR. FU MANCHU	(1668, $3.50)

By Mary Roberts Rinehart

THE HAUNTED LADY	(1685, $3.50)
THE SWIMMING POOL	(1686, $3.50)

By Ellery Queen

WHAT'S IN THE DARK	(1648, $2.95)

Available wherever paperbacks are sold, or order direct from the Publisher. Send cover price plus 50¢ per copy for mailing and handling to Zebra Books, Dept. 1766, 475 Park Avenue South, New York, N.Y. 10016. DO NOT SEND CASH.

THE BEST IN GOTHICS FROM ZEBRA

THE BLOODSTONE INHERITANCE   (1560, $2.95)
by Serita Deborah Stevens

The exquisite Parkland pendant, the sole treasure remaining to lovely Elizabeth from her mother's fortune, was missing a matching jewel. Finding it in a ring worn by the handsome, brooding Peter Parkisham, Elizabeth couldn't deny the blaze of emotions he ignited in her. But how could she love the man who had stolen THE BLOODSTONE INHERITANCE!

THE SHRIEKING SHADOWS OF
PENPORTH ISLAND   (1344, $2.95)
by Serita Deborah Stevens

Seeking her missing sister, Victoria had come to Lord Hawley's manor on Penporth Island, but now the screeching gulls seemed to be warning her to flee. Seeing Julian's dark, brooding eyes watching her every move, and seeing his ghost-like silhouette on her bedroom wall, Victoria knew she would share her sister's fate — knew she would never escape!

THE HOUSE OF SHADOWED ROSES   (1447, $2.95)
by Carol Warburton

Penniless and alone, Heather was thrilled when the Ashleys hired her as a companion and brought her to their magnificent Cornwall estate, Rosemerryn. But soon Heather learned that danger lurked amid the beauty there — in ghosts long dead and mysteries unsolved, and even in the arms of Geoffrey Ashley, the enigmatic master of Rosemerryn.

CRYSTAL DESTINY   (1394, $2.95)
by Christina Blair

Lydia knew she belonged to the high, hidden valley in the Rockies that her father had claimed, but the infamous Aaron Stone lived there now in the forbidding Stonehurst mansion. Vowing to get what was hers, Lydia would confront the satanic master of Stonehurst — and find herself trapped in a battle for her very life!

Available wherever paperbacks are sold, or order direct from the Publisher. Send cover price plus 50¢ per copy for mailing and handling to Zebra Books, Dept. 1766, 475 Park Avenue South, New York, N.Y. 10016. DO NOT SEND CASH.

TRIVIA MANIA: TV GREATS

TRIVIA MANIA: I LOVE LUCY	(1730, $2.50)
TRIVIA MANIA: THE HONEYMOONERS	(1731, $2.50)
TRIVIA MANIA: STAR TREK	(1732, $2.50)
TRIVIA MANIA: THE DICK VAN DYKE SHOW	(1733, $2.50)
TRIVIA MANIA: MARY TYLER MOORE	(1734, $2.50)
TRIVIA MANIA: THE ODD COUPLE	(1735, $2.50)

Available wherever paperbacks are sold, or order direct from the Publisher. Send cover price plus 50¢ per copy for mailing and handling to Zebra Books, Dept. 1766, 475 Park Avenue South, New York, N.Y. 10016. DO NOT SEND CASH.